CACTUS
CHRISTMAS

A TEXAS WINE TRAIL SERIES

≫ BOOK 1 ≪

CACTUS
CHRISTMAS

A TEXAS WINE TRAIL SERIES

≫ BOOK 1 ≪

Heather Renée May

MAYDAY PUBLISHING LTD

For special bulk discounts, or to arrange for the author to attend your live event, please visit the author's website, or address correspondence to: info@heatherreneemay.com

MayDay Publishing Ltd. Co.
2028 E Ben White Blvd #240-5666
Austin, TX 78741

Cover & Interior Design by the Book Cover Whisperer:
OpenBookDesign.biz

Chapter Illustrations by Victoria Horner
Editing & Proofreading through NYBookEditors
Line/Structural Editing by Megan McKeever
Copyediting by William Drennan
Headshot/Bio Photos by Abraham Rowe Photography

Library of Congress Control Number: 2021918930

978-1-7377193-0-4 Paperback
978-1-7377193-1-1 eBook

Manufactured in the United States of America

Printing & Distribution by Ingram Spark

FIRST EDITION

Dedicated to my sweet, brave, and loving Dotty.

⇾ Foreword ⇽

This book contains fictional characters, and any resemblance to persons living or dead is purely coincidental. However, the places in this book were real at the time of writing. The research for this book was done in 2020 on the Texas Wine Trail during the Covid-19 pandemic. Therefore, some restrictions prevented the author from tasting onsite and some liberties were taken. There are plenty more wineries not listed, and this book is not meant to be an exhaustive list of wine tours or wineries in the Texas Hill Country, but merely a taste.

Please go to texaswinetrail.com for a complete listing of participating wineries, and come visit this beautiful and unique Texas wine country for yourself.

Further, this book is not meant to be used as a guide for RV life. There are plenty of resources that are much more comprehensive than this that the author encourages you to explore.

⇉ One ⇇

EARLY OCTOBER

Kate woke up with a pounding headache and her throat dry. The room was dark save for the crack of light that shone through the hotel's blackout curtains. She rubbed her eyes and rolled over to her side. At eye level she could see the empty bottle of cheap wine and groaned at the memory of the day before.

She sat up and pushed herself back until she rested against the ruffled pillows and the stiff headboard. Kate felt at that moment that she didn't want to go on. Littered around the queen-size bed she could make out the remnants of the clothes and belongings she had thrown in bags heaped on the floor.

It wasn't supposed to be this way.

She looked down at her wedding band, and the diamond felt heavy against her swollen finger. Kate took a deep breath, letting her hand fall to rest lifeless against the bedspread coverlet.

The day before had held so much promise. She cringed with regret as she remembered how hopeful she had been anticipating the premiere of her husband's latest film. He was planning to leave that afternoon for the Salt Lake City Independent Film Festival, with Kate to join him the next day. Kate had been packing up their belongings while David was fielding phone calls from festival organizers all over the country.

She was proud of his work. A staunch proponent for investigative journalism, David had exposed some of the most heinous crimes against our natural world. He had won awards for his work on the poaching of sea turtles, and this latest work exposed the fishing industry and their part in contributing to the demise of our larger mammal friends whales, dolphins, and porpoises.

Kate had beamed to herself while folding his shirts into the open suitcase. At that moment she had felt extremely proud to be his wife. He could have chosen anyone, but he chose her.

Well, she laughed to herself, he chose her after she had sought him out as a mentor. He was twenty years her senior, she had followed his work all through journalism school, and he was a big reason she had pursued a career in writing.

Writing to expose, to share, to inform, to connect.

She had wanted her life to be more meaningful and to have an impact as well. Five years ago, when she saw that he was coming to teach a workshop on writing for film, Kate had jumped at the opportunity. She had booked a last-minute plane ticket to Charleston, flying from New York to spend the weekend in the hope that she would meet her idol.

She had secretly hoped that they would get to spend time alone.

Now, as Kate opened her eyes in the still darkened room, she thought, *Be careful what you wish for.*

Closing her eyes again she drifted back to the past. It had been a whirlwind romance. Dangerous and exciting. He was opinionated and strong, and Kate couldn't resist his charm and charisma. She also knew that others couldn't resist as well.

His phone would beep with text messages at all hours of the night. At one point she saw that they were from women's names she didn't know, all professing their love for him and saying they couldn't wait to see him again.

Kate had been out of her depth. David had insisted that they were nothing and that Kate was just insecure and jumping to conclusions. That she was the only one he loved. Yet there was this nagging sense of dread inside Kate's gut. Their long-distance relationship lasted a short eight months, when she finally gave up trying to compete for his attention. She had broken it off and cut communication.

Then, a few months later, they saw each other unexpectedly at the Houston/Intercontinental airport during a changeover. That weekend changed everything. David dangled the ultimate carrot: marriage. At forty-three, Kate didn't have any other prospects. It would be his third marriage and her first. She decided to take the chance and dive into the deep end. She believed that if she loved him enough he would change. That they could make this marriage work.

She remembered the ecstatic feeling of happiness as they forged a life together. She had never met anyone with whom she could laugh so deeply. However, instead of sharing a life, it was more a matter of Kate merging her life into his. He was entrenched in Charleston culture and history, with familial ties that prevented him from leaving. Kate packed up her life in New York and moved into his estate.

From the first moment she walked into his world, Kate knew that she was on unequal ground. He had everything in his life planned. He had housekeepers to take care of all his daily chores, and a staff to attend to his needs at the small office he ran from the guest cottage on the estate grounds.

With his deep roots in the area, he was well known and loved by everyone. As an outsider, Kate immediately struggled to find her place.

She had settled into the routine of his life, but she still felt something was off.

It was just then, as Kate had been organizing his socks, that she unzipped the side pouch in David's suitcase where she saw a piece of paper stuck inside. Her gut hummed as she gently pulled on the edge of the paper. It was a card with a colorful sea porpoise on it, and as she opened it, a picture fell out of a beautiful older woman in a bikini on a beach. Alarms went off in Kate's head, "To my hero, I'll never forget our time together and I'll wait here patiently for your return. Always, R."

Any excitement immediately vanished and was replaced by a deep knowing and heavy dread. It was one of the same women who had texted David before their breakup. One he promised he had severed ties with. Yet, this time, Kate knew that he had lied about it being over. That it had been nothing.

This was something.

She had heard a bustle in the hallway outside their bedroom and Kate impulsively shoved the card back into the zippered pocket. "Kate! Where are you? Come join us for a champagne toast, love!" Kate cringed and called back, "Be right there!"

You know those moments that completely change a trajectory or life path? This was Kate's moment. She knew intrinsically that she couldn't go back to playing the role of the devoted wife, knowing she wasn't enough. Knowing that there were lies and deceit just below the surface. She couldn't deny how she felt any longer. It didn't matter whether the affair was physical or emotional. The fact that David needed someone besides her made her realize that she would never truly make him happy. And he didn't seem to care if she was unhappy. He didn't want to change. He wanted what he wanted. He was the famous one. The legend. She was just a woman: expendable.

She had a choice: to shut up and continue to live this life of luxury and fame, having on the surface everything she ever needed; or to walk away from the limelight and the security of being married and take a chance on her own.

Some people live very well with denial. Not Kate. She preferred the truth, even if it was unpleasant.

She resolved that once he left for the airport, she would pack up her things for good.

Opening her swollen eyes back in that hotel room, Kate took a deep breath as she exhaled all of her dreams and hopes into the dark. She had made the ultimate choice: to leave. And she didn't have any real proof other than her gut and her moral compass.

Lord, only you can help me now.

Kate was alone again, fending for herself. She would forge ahead bravely without knowing what she might face in the future.

David had always told her that no one would

love her as he did. Maybe that was true. Kate swallowed the lump of grief rising in her throat and steeled herself. If this was the only kind of love she could get, then she would learn to live without. She didn't want crumbs.

She wanted the whole cake.

⇉ Two ⇇

Caroline was cleaning up her kitchen from Sunday's brunch when her phone rang. She dried her hands on the dish towel as she peered at the screen and said, "Kate."

"Darlin'! How ARE you? Are you in Salt Lake City yet?" she sang into the phone as she cradled it for a moment at her neck.

The voice on the other end was weak. "Not exactly." And Caroline heard her dear friend clear her throat with a cough before speaking again. Her normally strong and happy voice sounded ragged and broken.

"Um, Car . . ." She paused. "I've left David."

Caroline dropped the towel and held the phone upright to her ear. "Oh, no. What happened?"

For the next thirty minutes, Kate filled her in on the events from the day before.

Caroline was one of those friends who was more like a sister. It didn't matter how far away they lived, or what kind of life changes happened, they always seemed connected. Kate also appreciated that Caroline always had time to listen to her. She never felt rushed, and she took her advice to heart.

"Oh, sweet girl," Caroline stated sadly. "Are you sure you don't want to try and talk to him about it? Maybe there's a reasonable explanation . . ." she trailed off unconvincingly.

"No. We've been down this rabbit hole before. David always denies and tells me I'm making things up. Honestly, I don't think I will ever know for sure, but I'm tired of him manipulating the truth. I have to trust myself," she said firmly.

"Truthfully, from the beginning I should have known this would never change. He lives in a fast-paced, exciting world, where the values are a bit skewed. It's almost expected that someone with his kind of legacy would have multiple love interests. There certainly hasn't been a lack of admirers over the few years I've known him."

Kate thought about the social events, cocktails, and dinner parties that had been her life for the past few years. She cringed when she thought of what everyone would think. She was playing right into the critics' hands as the much younger wife, confirming that the marriage wouldn't last. She felt like she'd failed. She knew it was a big deal to choose this moment to walk away from him, when he was counting on her to be by his side. She also knew that she couldn't lie to herself any longer.

"The worst part is that I truly thought we would be this creative team and make this big splash in the documentary film world. I thought he really and truly wanted to do this with me. That he was as invested in my talent as he said he was.

"Instead of us working together to build a dream, I stepped into his world and watched my own dreams get set aside."

Caroline nodded in agreement, "Yes, I was worried that his fame would overshadow your spark. You've always had such a strong spirit and beautiful creativity, Kate. His flame could either add to yours, or you'd just be consumed."

Kate remembered how they had talked in the beginning about collaborating, but soon after they were married she saw this vision drifting out of view. She remembered pushing this and trying to get him to sit down to work with her on ideas. He had brushed her off and merely stated, "Why can't you just be?"

Kate had bristled at the comment and said, "But this is who I am. I am a writer, and I want to establish myself—my identity . . ." She had trailed off, frustrated in trying to explain, when he had merely said to her, "Why do you need an identity? Why can't you just be happy being my wife?"

Kate came back to the present and replied to her friend, "Exactly. I'm afraid that if I stay any longer, I'll lose that spark completely.

"Lately I've begun questioning who I am. What is my purpose?

"Do you know that I actually had the thought yesterday, as I was folding his freaking underwear, that maybe I should just be happy being his wife and not pursue my writing?" Kate grimaced as she said the words out loud.

Caroline exhaled loudly into the phone, "Oh, hell no. I would never let that happen, and neither would your agent. You owe her another book."

Kate knowingly nodded into the phone.

"I thought that marriage would be the final piece of the puzzle, making my life complete. Instead, I feel more lost than ever."

Kate paused for a moment and looked grimly around the hotel room.

"Where do I go now? Car, how will I recover from this?" Kate barely squeaked out.

Caroline took just a moment before responding, "Well, you *are* gonna get through this. You'll see, over time.

"Right now, though, maybe the best thing you can do is get yourself back into your work. Write, Kate."

Kate sighed deeply into the phone and said, "Well, I don't even know where to begin. I feel like I lost all my drive focusing on the 'us' of our marriage and partnership. You know my last book didn't do too well. But I have to come up with something to fulfill my contract."

Caroline interjected, "Girl. You ARE a writer. It's what you do. Just because you married a man doesn't mean you gave all of that away. Just because one book didn't do well doesn't mean you should give up." She took the tone of a cheerleader, "You need to get back in the saddle. And write!

"Are you just going to give up your dreams because of someone else's bad manners? Hell, Naw!" Caroline answered for her with a southern flourish at the end.

Kate nodded and laughed quietly. "Well, honestly, I've always wanted to write that fiction novel but never had the time to focus on it, what with David's relentless schedule. He also thought fiction was a waste of time."

"Oh, Gawd, what does he know? Write that novel, girl!" Caroline cheered.

Kate sat up a little straighter against the headboard. "Okay, let me reach out to my agent and see what she thinks. It's worth a try, anyway?

"I'll have to find a place to write it, though, where I can get away from the memories and truly focus," Kate thought out loud.

"Well, you know you're always welcome here in Pensacola, darlin'," Caroline drawled. "But I think maybe a change of scenery would do you good.

"Come to think of it, I've heard of this place in the Hill Country of Texas where you can rent an Airstream right off of the Texas Wine Trail. This is the new thing: glamping. Why don't you check it out and see if you can stay there for a few months to write?"

Kate's eyes opened as she felt hope for the first time in hours. "You know I've always loved Airstreams." She laughed, adding, "And, of course, wine."

"Yes! I'll send you the link to the place

CACTUS CHRISTMAS   21

through text. Call them. Get the heck out of Charleston and head west. It'll do you good to get away from everything you know, and spend time and energy on yourself for a change," Caroline said, pleased with herself.

"Okay. Yes. This is perfect. I'll go find a storage unit for my things and see how soon I can stay there."

Kate exhaled after realizing she'd been holding her breath. "Thank you so much for being there for me. I know that not many people will understand this separation, and I am so grateful for having you in my corner."

"Oh, phish. Who gives a rats you-know-what about them?" Caroline spewed into the phone. "Kate, you are worthy of having a wonderful life. You deserve happiness and freedom. And we need all of your creative talents.

"Get out there and find yourself again."

Kate smiled as she hung up. She closed her eyes for a moment, picturing what it would be like staying in an Airstream in Texas. She heard a ping from her phone and opened her eyes to see the link of the RV park come over text: "Open Air Resorts, Spicewood, TX."

She took a deep breath and clicked through to call for a reservation, telling herself that she was doing the right thing, even if it was confusing and painful. It was now or never. And truly, time would tell.

———

HALF AN HOUR LATER, Kate clicked her phone off. It was done. She had made a reservation for one of the Airstreams. The lady on the other end of the line had a carefree and friendly demeanor. Kate hoped that she could feel that way again someday. Perhaps Texas was going to give her the change in perspective that she needed?

She pushed back the heavy hotel curtains, and bright light stole into the room. The window faced the asphalt parking lot framed by a few beautiful tall old oak trees. Kate had one more piece of the puzzle to fit. She had to convince her agent to take a chance. Changing genres was risky. Kate felt that she didn't have much to lose after the last book's flop. Perhaps it was fate telling her that she was meant to write something different all along?

She'd never know until she tried. Truthfully, she didn't want to write anything that was set in fact. She wanted to hide behind fictional characters and dive into a world that would help her escape from her own reality. She was tired of trying to uncover the truth. Truth may be stranger than fiction, but fiction is more believable.

Kate used to love telling stories. In fact, when she was younger, her mother would take Kate and her sister, Lillie, for long drives along the coast.

The Olympic Peninsula stretched out before them as they wound around in and out of forests with the Strait of Juan de Fuca tempting just beyond. They would pass an old house and make up stories about the people who lived there. Maybe it would be a house. Or a car. Or an old farm building. Kate delighted in those tales, and continued to build on the stories long after they had moved onto the next one.

Back to the present, Kate vowed to go back and find that girl again. To find the fun and joy of those stories and the magic they contained.

She picked up her phone again and called her agent.

Margaret picked up on the second ring. "Well, hello there! How's my favorite author?"

Kate grimaced, wondering what she'd think after she heard what she had to say.

"I am embarking on a new journey of sorts, and I'd like to pitch you an idea for my next book"—she hesitated—"er, novel."

Margaret picked up the thread immediately, "Wait, are you thinking you want to write fiction?"

Kate hesitated for a moment before fully committing, "Yes."

She then quickly dove into all the reasons and justifications; her separation from David, her last flop, her need to find something she could really be inspired by.

"I'm hoping that this will help me to tap back into my love for writing, and maybe help me to heal a bit as well in the process," she finished on her last breath.

The line was silent save for Margaret processing this information with a few audible hmms.

She finally spoke. "Changing genres is usually a risky endeavor. With anyone else, I would advise against it. Yet, with you, Kate, you are still building up your following. Certainly your first work was impressive. But I have to agree, your heart was not in your second."

Kate swallowed hard.

"Give me a day or two and let me pitch this to the publisher. I think that with the new angle, and your change in circumstance, this may just work out."

"Thank you, Margaret."

"Listen, don't thank me, just get writing. If we are going to do this, we have to pitch hard and deliver fast. I want your draft on my desk by the end of the year. Can you do that?"

"I don't really have a choice," Kate replied. "Yes."

"Excellent. Okay, let me get to work on this and I'll get back to you." She paused for a moment. "And Kate? I'm sorry to hear about everything with David."

Kate could feel her eyes begin to burn, "Thanks, Margaret. I appreciate that."

"Who knows? Maybe this is just what you need to get fully back in the saddle? I know you have it in you, Kate. Now get cracking!"

Kate felt encouraged as she clicked off her phone again. *That's it, then* she thought. *Guess it's time to head to Texas.*

By making a few pivotal decisions, she was changing the direction of her life overnight. Was it that simple?

It didn't feel simple to Kate. It felt enormous and insurmountable. She was determined, though, and now she had a purpose.

⇉ Three ⇇

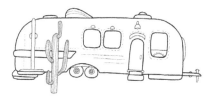

NOVEMBER

The dark of night began to gradually wane as pastel shades of sunrise took over the sky's easel. Whispers of clouds fingered the horizon while Kate sat in her trailer, sipping her first cup of the day. She looked at the microwave clock: 6:00 a.m. It was the time of year when the days got much shorter, leaving her many mornings wide awake in the pitch black, anxiously waiting for her day to begin. She took another sip of French roast and pondered her situation.

Sitting in a rented Airstream trailer in the Hill Country of Texas, she regarded the shiny box with appreciation. A forty-two-foot metal time capsule she would spend her next few months inside of, hammering away on her keyboard. She heard her neighbors' coughs emerging from the pop-up trailer next door. The sun was gaining traction as the colors turned from pink to yellow, despite the moon still hanging high, refusing to give up the night.

The past week had left Kate exhausted. While David was away, she quickly found a unit in Charleston to store her few belongings: mementos, artwork, extra clothes, books, and other treasures from her past. She couldn't bring herself to go back to the house. It was too painful, and also too easy for her to change her mind. No. It was time Kate stood up for herself and her writing. To become the writer

CACTUS CHRISTMAS   ❧ 31

she'd always thought she would be. To carve out her future and prove something to herself. That she was better than settling for less. She had driven nearly nonstop on adrenaline until she had arrived in the Texas sunshine.

She had no idea what she would write. Procrastination, and maybe a healthy dose of fear-laced perfectionism, had kept her from writing this novel these past few years. Now, without having her joint account with David to rely on, she had to produce something to sustain herself. And quickly. Caroline was right: a change of scenery was just the nudge Kate needed to kick-start her creative juices. Being situated on the Wine Trail? That was just an added bonus. *I need all the inspiration I can get*, she thought.

Six years ago, Kate had her first book published. It was a smashing success, hitting the *New York Times* best-seller list in its first week and carrying her all over the country on a successful book tour.

Her second? A total flop. Heavily criticized by the media, it made her question her own validity as an author. The impostor syndrome took hold. Kate wondered if her first book was a fluke.

She met David soon after, and he gave her a perfect reason to let her writing take a backseat to his exciting life. He applauded her talent and then in the same breath told her it was okay for her not to write. That they would be a creative team. She hid her own inner promptings and got lost in the heady excitement of it all. Marriage seemed to be the perfect solution to validate her as a creative person and to allow her to focus solely on his empire.

Now, as she sat in the trailer, she could hide from her fears no longer. Draining her cup, Kate opened up her laptop and logged in. She stared at the empty white screen and took a deep breath. *They're just words*, she thought, *you know words. You can't be afraid of words.* She began pecking away toward her daily word count while the sun rose steadily above the line of trees.

It was much later when Kate sat back and stretched her arms above her head. Two thousand words and she was ready for a break. She had finally broken past her own barriers and had let the rhythm of her typing take over. Feeling a sense of satisfaction she hadn't felt in years, she scrolled through the pages, reading through some of the bits. *Don't*, she thought. *Don't self-edit. It's not time for that yet*. She did, however, check her overall word count: twenty thousand. It was a start.

Kate beamed with pride as she closed the laptop. She checked her iPhone, which had been put on silent so as not to distract her. A text reminder of her allergy prescription refill ready for pickup at the local CVS. Some junk email notifications. And multiple gray bubbles of missed calls from David and a text. The angry words seemed to jump off the screen at her.

"Why haven't you called me back? You know it's just like you . . ."

She gulped as she unlocked the phone to see the entire message.

". . . to run away and not deal with this. You have a responsibility to this marriage. It's just like you to leave me when I need you most. Everyone thinks you are selfish for not supporting me. I am your husband, and I deserve more respect than this."

Kate felt the cold slap across her face and felt a mixture of guilt and anger. She fumed at how she was considered the selfish one for leaving. Never mind his secret side life! It didn't matter, though; any argument he would turn in his favor, as he was a master at manipulating situations. He had too much of his ego invested in being right. They would just go round and round until she finally gave up. She would never win at his game.

Maybe she was being selfish for wanting

her freedom? She couldn't stand her own sec-
ond-guessing of the situation anymore.

She firmly turned the phone over facedown
on the table and slid out from the dinette booth.
It was so against her nature not to respond to
him. She was used to the role of the "fixer," the
one who made it all better. Yet, deep down, Kate
knew that she needed to unlearn that habit. To
truly find out who she was, she would have to
stand firm and on her own.

Taking a few deep breaths, she forced herself to stretch and breathe out all the negative
thoughts. They wouldn't help her to write and
only further stunt her creativity.

Standing, Kate brought herself back to the
present and looked around her, grateful to be
out of Charleston. She was surprised at how
she was adjusting to the narrow confines of
this tin can. It suited her well. All she needed
for the next few months was squirreled away in
whatever storage space she could find. This was

her buffer zone. Only Caroline knew where she was, and she trusted her. It was a safe place for her to focus on her work. The fact that this was a trailer gave her that whiff of travel without actually moving.

Kate used to love travel. Spontaneous road trips to check out a dive diner. Cruising on the highways and byways across the United States. She had loved that early part of her marriage, when they had been happy and carefree, roaming around scouting locations for his next film shoot. But forced travel can quickly become tedious. She grew tired of the La Quintas, instant coffee, and monotony of the daily miles. Additionally, she had felt more disconnected with her writing as David's work schedule took precedence over her creative inspiration.

Kate shook off the dusty memory and glanced back at the clock: 11:30 a.m. She needed to stop thinking about him, get out of the trailer, and explore. The great thing about wineries is that the tasting rooms open and close early. It is a given that you must start early if you want to get all the vineyards in. Drinking wine before noon? That's just good planning.

She looked at her Texas Wine Trail map and decided on her attack: she would hit the farthest one out, to arrive closer to home by the end of the day. She smiled, thinking of her favorite quote by Edward Albee, "Sometimes it's necessary to go a long distance out of the way to come back a short distance correctly."

Grabbing her leather tote, she placed her small orange notebook and a thin Sharpie pen inside. She had to be prepared to capture any moments of inspiration that might emerge between tastings. She pulled her blond locks up into a messy bun and fetched her aviator sunglasses before stepping out of the trailer, leaving her work and laptop behind. The dry heat instantly embraced her as she emerged into the fullness of day.

Open Air RV Resort was newly built and designed to attract remote tech workers as well as snowbirds desiring a different experience close to Austin. There were spots for RVs as well as tent camping, a brand- new clubhouse with tennis courts, and an open pool. She heard dogs barking across the way in the fenced- in park, and saw neighbors waving at one another as a Tiffin Motorhome pulled slowly through on the way out. A leader in environmental landscape, the park had natural patches of grass inter-spersed with stickers and cactus. The best part— six spots were reserved for guests like herself who wanted the glamper lifestyle without hav-ing to purchase a trailer. Bright, beautiful, retro, and new Airstreams stood proudly. Each had private patio areas with umbrella awnings and outdoor lighting. The red and turquoise colors contrasted with bright silver metal, creating a stunning and inspired view.

Caroline had told her, "Girl, if you can't write

a novel in this place, then you might as well give it up. Sunshine? Check. Glamper? Check. Wine? Check. Cowboys? Double-check." She had laughed, adding, "Heck, I may have to join you!"

Kate made a mental note to touch base with her friend. But first? Wine.

She got into her white Dodge Durango, revved the engine, and adjusted the air conditioning. Patsy Cline came out of her radio, "Crazy, I'm crazy for feeling so lonely . . ." *Darn right*, she thought. Kate eased out of her spot and then pulled onto Highway 290.

The windy two-lane highway reminded Kate of New Mexico. Twisting and turning through cactus- and sagebrush-covered hills. She could almost imagine the coyotes hiding out with their unflinching, sharp eyes.

She loved driving. It gave her a sense of control. That she was actually going somewhere, doing something. The jagged rock formations were like Braille to her eyes, unlocking all the secrets of the past. She wondered about those stories. How the settlers managed to "tame" this land and chose to live here in the dry wildness of it all.

The sun was golden bright, and Kate could almost taste the crispness in the air. She realized as she drove how much of her life she'd spent on autopilot. Job. School. Career. More school. She had assumed that marriage was the natural progression to this track. Followed by children. Isn't this what we are taught will bring meaning and fulfillment to our lives?

However, Kate's path took a sharp detour just as she was about to start her master's degree. She was single, in her early forties, and suffering from severe fibroids. Kate was forced to make the difficult choice to undergo a hysterectomy. She had channeled all of her loss into her writing. Determined to find meaning for her life even as it veered farther away from a conventional course.

When she met David, in some way it made sense. An unconventional marriage for her un-conventional life. She thought that somehow through her own unfortunate circumstances, she had been given an opportunity to validate herself and her life through this union.

Kate laughed ruefully to herself as she slowed down the car and pulled off the high-way into a dusty, dirt parking lot.

A voice inside her said, *Don't ever let anyone else define you.*

Kate turned off the ignition and made a pledge to herself: live life fully. She would no longer do what she "should," or what she thought "others" expected of her. She would no longer try to orchestrate the story of her own life, forcing the pieces to fit. Instead, she would venture down that mysterious and unknown road to embrace her true potential and purpose. She would have to swallow her own fear and do the hard work of allowing herself to grow and be discovered.

God, I know you are listening. I'm not going to try to do this by myself anymore. She held up her hands. *You get the reins.*

⇒ Four ⇐

The Texas Heritage Vineyard is just off Highway 290 and right before you hit the main street hustle and bustle of downtown Fredericksburg. Unassuming from the front, just two ranch-style buildings and a dusty parking lot set back a matter of yards from the winding highway.

Kate pulled into the parking lot, watching a couple leave the tasting room hand in hand with the glow that only drinking multiple glasses of wine in this kind of atmosphere can produce.

Once inside, Kate took in the tall ceilings, the bright wooden finishes, circular bar, and merchandise shop. She walked through the building to step outside onto the new deck overlooking the hills.

The view was spectacular. Half of the deck was covered with a vaulted tin roof separated by a beautiful stone chimney. She took a few steps down to the side deck, which boasted a bright yellow canvas awning to further shield from the midday sun.

The wind played gently across the taught canvas. A clean palate with which to start her tastings. She was poured a 2019 Riesling and could taste the Granny Smith apple and pear in the fruit forward crisp white.

She stood leaning against the wooden railing, taking in the rolling hills beyond. A herd of deer made their way up to a feeder and lounged about, taking refuge from the sun under a cluster of oak trees. Kate was pondering their innocence when she saw a flash of blue out of the corner of her eye. She turned her head slightly, shielding her eyes from the sunlight's glare to regard the interruption.

"Do you mind if I share this view?" a man asked as he sidled up to the railing with a half-filled glass of what appeared to be a cabernet. Kate's eyes went from his deep blue Brooks Brothers vest to the glass of wine and traveled up to finally rest on his tanned face. He smiled at her, and laugh lines danced around the most piercing blue eyes she'd seen.

Instantly attracted, she laughed at herself for a moment before responding, "Of course. This is a view that should be shared." She took another sip of her wine a bit more self-consciously and then turned back to take in the beauty of the Hill Country herself.

"You know, I haven't been out here for years. It's honestly even more beautiful than I remem-bered." He gave a reminiscent nod to the hills.

Intrigued, she asked, "What's kept you away?"

He shrugged slightly, keeping his eyes on the horizon. "Well, life, I suppose."

He paused as the hostess came up to them with two opened bottles and poured them each their respective next tastings. A 2019 Voignier for Kate, made with locally sourced grapes from the Wildseed Farms. She swirled the clear liquid gently and took a sip, instantly greeted by the silky, smooth stone fruit. Midway through her second sip, she could taste hints of honeysuckle. She watched with curiosity as the woman was pouring him a luscious-looking deep red.

"This is the 2017 Alicante Bouschet. Full of pepper notes, tobacco, leather grown from the Lahey Vineyard in the High Plains. A perfect wine to sip by the fire on a chilly night." She winked at them both and turned to head to the next group of tasters a few tables away.

The man placed his glass on the wooden

railing and swirled the wine somewhat vigorously. "Best way to really open up some of these reds."

Kate watched him sip as he continued, "Yes, that is a very robust one. I've been up in the Northeast for years now, but I graduated from UT and always intended to return to establish my practice." He laughed to himself somewhat regretfully. "That didn't exactly happen. Crazy how life can take you for a ride."

He turned to smile at her, and she felt her knees wobble for a hot second. Clearing her throat, she responded, "Yes, I definitely know that feeling. One minute you think you are going in a set direction, and then the map changes." She turned to him. "You are here now, though." And with that, she held up her glass and they toasted.

Kate tried to determine his age. If she had to guess, it would be about hers. It was rare for her to meet anyone her age, let alone someone so outright handsome and easy to talk to. She assumed he was married—the good ones always are. They stood there for a moment, both just taking in the scene. A few birds swooped playfully by. In the distance, a turkey vulture took a break from scavenging to soar the warm air in large arcs.

The man finished his wine and lifted the empty glass into the sunlight. "Beautiful. Tastes like Texas." He smiled at her. "I don't mean to take up your time. Thank you for letting me enjoy this."

Kate turned sideways to him. "You're not interrupting anything. In fact, I welcome the distraction." He turned toward her, seemingly interested, so she continued, "I have a bit of writer's block and am up against a deadline. So I figured a little wine and a change of scenery would help." She nodded to the hills as she raised her glass.

"Ah," he stated knowingly. "Yes, I've found

much inspiration in these hills over the years. I find there is something truly beautiful about this landscape; rugged, strong, and yet pure."

She smiled at him. "I like the way you put that."

"Well, I'm no writer, but I try." He grinned at her before letting his gaze get distracted by a small doe making her way to a feeder in the field below.

Kate followed his gaze. "They are so beautiful and helpless," she said somewhat sadly. "I wish I could protect them from what lurks in these hills."

"Oh, I bet they do a pretty good job of protecting themselves." He added, "I imagine they can outsmart those coyotes. Safety in numbers."

He turned away for a moment and she watched the silhouette of his sturdy, solid frame out of the corner of her eye. She wondered about his story. He turned back to face her, and Kate's heart skipped a quick beat.

"You know, I'm planning on visiting a few wineries for tastings this week. If you are interested, I'd love to have your company. Perhaps I can help you with your writer's block, and you can help me find the right winery to invest in?" he asked.

"Well, I'm certainly no wine expert, but I know what I like." She smiled.

"I'm no expert at words, but sometimes the best advice can come from those with the least experience," he countered.

Kate's smile grew wide as she agreed. "Then this sounds like a perfect arrangement."

He stuck his hand out. "Zach."

She fit her hand into his warmth. "Kate."

Zach pulled a folded paper map out of his pocket and Kate recognized the 290 Wine Trail.

"Do you have a plan in mind?" she asked him as she took another sip of her wine.

"Sort of." He smiled sideways at her and laughed in a way that was immediately endearing to Kate. "I have sketched out fifteen to twenty wineries I have some interest in, with a few of them that I definitely want to check out."

Zach ran his long, slender finger against the thin map line and traced it along, circling as he pointed out his route. "But, you know, that can all change depending on local intel. I decided to take a sort of business/organic approach to this search." He turned to her, "Mostly I just want to enjoy having a much-needed break and be inspired at the same time."

Kate not only loved a distraction, but she really loved to explore. To be able to have a reason to visit, discover, and compare wineries she had never been to. It would likely have been too intimidating for her alone, but having someone to pal along with gave her a welcome sense of comfort.

She finished the last of her wine and set the glass on the table opposite the railing.

"Ready?" Zach asked.

"You bet. Let's wine it up!" She laughed at her rather lame joke and he motioned for her to lead as they made their way out to the parking lot and followed each other to their first destination.

Kate could hardly contain her excitement and disbelief as she followed his silver Range Rover a short distance down Highway 290. *How on earth? Maybe all this talk about embracing life and stating your intentions really works?* She laughed as she adjusted the air conditioning. *Well, he's only here for a week, and I honestly have a novel to write. Besides, there's no way he's really interested in me.* The last time she felt this kind of instant attraction seemed like ages ago. What a great diversion, though. Without even trying, she had made a new friend and partner in crime. There are worse ways to spend time than getting to hang out with such a handsome fellow. She felt like she had just stepped into a Hallmark movie. As he turned into the next parking lot, she coached herself to just enjoy each moment and not to try to figure out where it leads. It's just wine and company.

Pulling into a spot next to his, she cut her engine and grabbed her bag. Fueled by the tingling sensation of wine and anticipation, she stepped out of her car and fell into step with him.

⇉   Five   ⇇

The Bingham Family Vineyards is a stone's throw from Texas Heritage. Just off the highway, this building is much larger than the previous winery and next to the Yee Haw Ranch Outfitter. A fine gravel parking lot blankets the prominent twin gray barns. Inside, Kate and Zach took in the magnitude of the space. Beautifully stained wood extended high into the bright vaulted ceiling. A dramatic wrought iron chandelier hung down over the enormous tasting bar that encircled most of the main room. The sides of the bar were affixed with sheets of imprinted metal, and a brown leather saddle stood prominently on the long table in the middle.

Zach and Kate took a spot at the counter and looked through the list of tasting options. Reds and whites organized by degree of sweet- ness. "You can choose five of our wines for ten dollars, or fifteen dollars for all reds," the sommelier suggested.

Kate turned to Zach. "Which do you prefer? I gravitate toward the dry palate."

He nodded in agreement. "Yes, that and very bold reds. The bolder the better." He pointed to the list. "I've been wanting to try their Cabernet Sauvignon. All these wines are produced from grapes grown in the High Plains."

The sommelier nodded. "Yes, that area is southwest of the Panhandle, and with the dry elevation and cool nights, these grapes produce wines with a wonderful natural balance of sugar and acid."

Kate shrugged. "Well, I am a novice at tasting." She laughed, then added, "Not of drinking, of course. This will be a real treat for me to pick your brain about Texas wines."

He smiled back at her, somewhat embarrassed. "Yes, I have been sort of obsessed with Texas wine knowledge these past few years. I apologize if I overshare. But you'll give me an excuse to dust off my elevator pitch and see what sticks."

They both laughed as Kate decided, "We'll do the reds."

A steady cacophony of conversations bounced and echoed off the barn walls. As they made their way to a side table in the tasting room, Kate realized how easily Zach moved. He seemed very comfortable with himself and she pondered ever so briefly about what he might look like underneath his vest. She blushed as she caught him staring back at her, as if he could read her mind.

Clearing her throat, she quickly refocused. "So, tell me about this obsession of yours?"

He settled into his chair and swirled his wine a bit before taking a sip. "Well, I have been entertaining this sort of side project. It really began about five years ago." He paused for another sip. "Wow, this is a really nice blend."

Kate nodded. "Yes, I'm not exactly sure of the proper wording, but I love the deep, almost cherry notes." He agreed. She liked that he didn't try to correct or "teach" her, but instead let her just discover each new taste on her own.

He continued, "Some buddies from school invited me down for a weekend of golf and to visit local wineries. I had been so focused on my career that I hadn't taken much time to just blow off steam. But that trip was sort of transformative for me." He laughed. "Well, maybe not for my golf game; I am still a solid bogey golfer. But in the way that I fell back in love with this part of the country again."

She nodded. She loved listening to his smooth voice. "So, we were drinking Scotch one night by the fire and reminiscing about our school days. Back when we didn't have so many responsibilities. Back when we weren't adulting. And that's when we started throwing around this idea that someday we should come back here and start a winery together."

He finished his glass of Cabernet and set it gently back down on the table. Kate was completely intrigued. "I love that idea. Imagine"— she motioned her arm to take in the whole room—"this could all be yours. I wonder how much work it actually takes to run one of these wineries. I mean, aren't they mostly associated with large, multigenerational families?"

"Yes, mostly. Which is why this idea surfaced in our group, as one of my buddies' family runs a vineyard northeast of here and has a lot of knowledge about this lifestyle."

Kate sipped her Cabernet thoughtfully. "Lifestyle. That certainly is a way to describe it. Seems so romantic. And free."

"Yes, that freedom is definitely a draw." He paused, growing a bit more serious. "I really think I've lost so much of my own sense of freedom over the years. I have lived my life as I was expected. I went through my schooling all the way through my doctorate, then up to Boston for my residency, and now I have a private practice I share with four other doctors."

Kate was impressed, "Wow. I totally understand where you are coming from. I mean, not medical school, but the idea of feeling locked into a charted course in life." Her eyes connected with his. "What type of practice?"

"General, or family practice. I really didn't want to specialize, as that would require more schooling and honestly I was ready to just start seeing patients."

They were interrupted by the sommelier as he brought them a final tasting in their red flight. Once they sniffed and swirled, they each took a sip, raising their eyebrows across the table at each other and catching a moment of easy agreement.

Kate wasn't sure how Zach felt, but she was already getting warm inside and was surprised at how comfortable she was in his presence. "So, from blood to wine, eh?" she said as he laughed in response.

"I suppose so. I guess I began to escape a bit in my mind, thinking about what I really wanted." He looked squarely in her eyes. "Do you ever feel like you've been living a life that isn't yours?"

Kate gulped as that remark hit directly home. "Absolutely. I feel like I've spent most of my life trying to do what I think other people expect of me. At some point—and maybe people call this the midlife crisis— you wake up and think, *What do I have to show for all this? And am I truly happy?*"

His eyes sparkled a bit in recognition of this longing they both shared. "Happiness. What is that, really?" He took another sip. "I mean, isn't that selfish to want to be happy? At least that's how I was raised, to give selflessly to others and that should be enough."

Kate nodded emphatically. "Oh, yes. I am quite aware of that mind-set. In fact, that sort of thinking is what got me into my sort of doomed-from-the-start marriage."

Kate grimaced slightly before explaining. "I thought that I could hide my own needs underneath the blanket of marriage and that would be enough." She quickly looked up at him as he remained silent. "It's not that I didn't want to be married or devoted. It's just that I guess I sort of short-changed my own hopes and dreams in the process."

Zach nodded. "I understand completely. My wife, or should I say, ex-wife and I divorced five years ago." Kate looked up at him hopefully as she recognized that he had already been down the road she was just getting ready to take.

"How did you survive?" she blurted out and then let the words float down softly.

Zach held her gaze and responded, "Time. Honestly, that is what it has taken." He took another sip of his wine. "Also, we had a pretty amicable split, thankfully. She was just as miserable as I. We were both chasing some sort of dream our families had laid out for us generations before." He looked plainly at her. "We just really weren't happy in the end, no matter how hard we tried. I'm really sorry to hear you are going through this, though," he added.

Kate fingered the wedding band on her finger and shrugged. "Thank you. It wasn't a long marriage, but it certainly had a great impact. And the process is only a few months along now."

"Well, hang in there," he added encouragingly. "It will get better. It was superhard for us at first, but we made a point to stay friendly for our daughter Chloe's sake."

"That's good," Kate said a bit enviously. "How old is she now?"

"Seventeen," he replied with pride. "Part of why I feel I can finally leave the Northeast soon. As long as she gets settled into college. Of course, I'm hoping she'll choose my alma mater, UT" He smirked at her and said, "Hook 'em, Horns!" Zach extended his pinkie and index finger and shook it, catching her eyes sparkling as they laughed and broke up the somber moment. "You can take the guy out of Texas . . ." He trailed off as he pushed his chair away and stood. "Seems like a good time to head for our next tasting?"

He reached out his hand to her as she grabbed her tote, rising on the strength of his arm. Pulling closer to him, she caught a whiff of his aftershave and couldn't tell if it was that or standing that made her dizzy. They waved to the sommelier and headed out to their cars toward the next destination, Longhorn Cellars.

———

"Now, THIS IS A Texas winery landscape if I ever saw one," Kate stated as she raised her tasting of 2018 Voignier to eye level, seeing the longhorn cattle graze through the top of her clear glass.

Longhorn Cellars is a boutique winery across Highway 290 and just up a pace from Bingham. Specializing in Terroir wines, each of their three locations offered wines with a unique expression of the Hill Country American Viticultural Area, showing how using the same grapes, each wine from their three regions, were different depending on the microclimate, soil, and water.

By this time they had settled into a lovely

rhythm. Taste. Ponder. Discuss. Enjoy the scenery. It all seemed as fluid as each wine that was poured into their expectant glasses. Kate was amazed at how they had opened up to each other in a relatively short time. *Perhaps it's easier to talk to strangers about difficult things*, she pondered.

Zach turned to her. "I've been going on and on about me. What brought you to this beautiful country?"

Outside, they were sitting underneath canvas shade awnings in comfortable lounge chairs low to the ground. Kate settled back into her chair. "Well, I'm an author," she said somewhat flatly.

"Really?" he said with piqued interest.

"Don't get too impressed. My first book did really well, but now I'm working on my third and wondering why I'm doing this." She half laughed to herself as he nodded for her to explain. "I wonder whether that first book wasn't pure luck. I had a great publicist and a fantastic book tour. When I tried writing the second it fell completely flat."

She shrugged off the claustrophobic feeling. "Now, to fulfill my contract, I'm taking a huge risk by writing the fiction novel I've always wanted to. I needed to find a place filled with just enough inspiration and solitude to make that happen."

She raised her glass. "And a little distraction and healing in the form of wine isn't a bad idea either." She winked at him. "If it doesn't go well, at least I'll have a good time writing it."

Zach laughed easily, "Oh, don't be so modest. I'm sure it will be amazing. And good for you for going for what you have always wanted."

Kate blushed and took a sip of her wine while he continued.

"I've often wondered what it's like to be an author. I mean, I have my entire path and routine charted out for me, down to every last detail. But as an author, you probably don't even know the world you will be writing about until it happens?"

"Well, I do try to chart out some plot lines, or I follow an initial inspiration. But after I start, the characters usually take on a life of their own and I feel like I'm just taking a ride on a bucking bronco." She finished her glass and added, "Besides, that's the best way—uncharted territory. I mean, if you always know everything that will happen to you forward and backward, where is the fun?"

He nodded wearily. "Exactly. I suppose it all becomes duty." He thought for a moment. "What do you think is more important, a life filled with duty or passion?"

She looked at him. "You are kidding, right? Of course I gravitate to passion a hundred percent. But honestly, there is a balance to strike there. I find that without some kind of routine, responsibility, or sense of duty, life can become very self-focused." She swirled the new fresh red liquid in her glass. "Actually, I take this back a bit, because even if you are duty-bound, you can actually be living very selfishly as well. I mean, on the surface to others you are doing what is expected of you and proving your worth in this world, but isn't that just as self-serving?" She raised her eyebrow to him as a challenge.

"Wow. Yes, I could absolutely see that. I know many people, myself included, who have used their jobs, their duty to feel better about themselves," he said. "It's likely why so many people stay busy all the time, because they can't stand to be alone with themselves. All that white noise. All that insecurity."

She toasted him on that. "We are really a culture of comparison and insecurity for sure. Like we can't think for ourselves until we check Facebook to compare our life with others or get validation from our friends."

He laughed. "Don't even get me started on

social media. I've avoided it for years, but my daughter and her friends are totally hooked." He shook his head. "It's really sad. They will never know what it's like to live life without a cell phone or the internet."

"Right!" Kate said emphatically. "I mean, I remember rotary phones and having to wait for my turn to call my friends to make play dates."

He laughed. "Yes. It's easy for every generation to say, 'those were the days,' but honestly it was a simpler time. We just knew to come home when the streetlights came on."

She took another sip, thinking about how lovely it was to talk with someone of her own generation.

Finding bonds in familiar references. Much of her past was straddling years of difference to find a common thread. Her husband had older children and grandchildren. Without kids of her own, Kate had thought this would give her a sense of belonging and finally fitting in.

That desire completely backfired. She ended up feeling even more like a piece of extra baggage in his world.

Zach interrupted her thoughts. "I just worry about my daughter and her sense of self. This phenomenon of finding validation through external means is honestly frightening."

"I think that's why I like writing so much," Kate agreed. "It's private. Something I do without anyone knowing until I'm ready for them to see. No instant gratification."

He nodded thoughtfully, leaning forward a bit in his chair. "But, of course, we are human and need some sort of validation of our purpose and worth, right?"

"Of course! But I think that the difference is that now people announce what they are doing and get that instant feedback before ever fully allowing the thoughts to mature. It's like we want the prize without the work."

He laughed out loud. "Oh, yes. A sense of

entitlement for sure. That if I have this great idea then I must be rewarded for it immediately."

They took a break to sip another selection and then let the silence fill the space between them. They could hear birds brightly chirping in the background and quiet conversation between couples on the other side of the open fence.

A white dog with black eye patches made her way through the opening at the bottom and began to beg for attention from a couple a few seats away.

Kate's voice broke through the dry air, "You know what this means, though? By indulging this need for validation, we are not allowing ourselves to grow. Like, we need to be perfect so badly that there is no room for failure."

Zach nodded. "Absolutely. I see these young doctors come out and they are completely ter- rified of doing something wrong. Don't get me wrong, I'm a doctor; we have a higher expec- tation of being perfect than others. But," he added, "we are fallible, and this is how we learn. Without failure, there is no growth."

"Exactly. As long as we are trying to keep up this air of perfection, we are making our own levels of anxiety go up because there is no way anyone can be perfect," she added, laughing. "And why would you want to be? How boring!"

They laughed together. "Another reason why prescriptions for antianxiety medications keep going up," he stated, changing the tone.

Kate shook her head, then lifted her glass again and motioned for him to look around. "And this is why we need good conversation, great wine, and beautiful scenery. They soothe the soul." Her eyes sparkled as they regarded each other.

Kate could feel the warmth rising in her cheeks but didn't care. She felt like she could bask in this moment forever. It had been so long since she had felt a true connection with a man like this, and she was immediately grateful in that moment. This was the salve for her soul.

They finished up their round and together looked at the map for the next destination, Fiesta Winery 290. His hand brushed against hers as they folded the map back up and she felt an electric shiver up her spine.

Pulling her hand away quickly, she fumbled with her bag for a moment, attempting to pull herself together. *Seriously, Kate*, she thought, *control yourself!*

As they walked to the parking lot, Zach stated, "Why don't I drive to the next place? I think this is probably the last one I can physically do today. Maybe we can grab something to eat and then I'll bring you back to your car after?"

Kate gulped at the prospect of sitting even closer to him for any period of time. "Yes, sure," she said weakly, and then added more boldly, "I will be ready to eat a horse after all this wine!"

When she climbed into the passenger seat of

his Range Rover, the soft brown leather felt like butter. She noticed how clean the rental was, and delighted in the new car smell. Enveloped in the cocoon of the car just inches away from touching his shoulders, Kate felt like the luckiest girl in the world. *Maybe Christmas was coming early after all?*

———

ARRIVING JUST A few moments later, they made their way through the stone courtyard to the entrance of the tasting room. The cobbled limestones of the walkway were warm yellow and worn from age and traffic. The courtyard was settled between a cluster of smaller wooden buildings. One housed a cute boutique shop, which, if Kate was on her own, she would have made a beeline to check out. Another building looked to be a private residence, and then the tasting room flanked the rear with a long, covered patio with wrought iron tables that spilled out to fill in the space. Kate found a couple of seats on either side of an overturned wine barrel, and Zach returned with the menu for their tasting.

"I just want to buy these bottles to put in my Airstream for decoration!" she exclaimed to Zach as she looked through the list with colorful, fun names.

"I'll try the Tex Way Rosé to start," she decided after much contemplation. She reached into her purse to pull out her wallet, but he stopped her, "Nope. I'll get this one, and how about you get the next?" She agreed, and sat back to take in the scenery while he went inside to fetch their selections.

Glancing around the courtyard, she could see the flat paddle-shaped cactus jutting out from cracks in the limestone wall. The sunlight was full and bright, but they sat in the cool shadows of the ranch-style patio.

Zach returned with two glasses and settled onto the barstool across from Kate. "Tell me about this Airstream," he asked as he took a sip of his '18 Voignier.

She tasted her Tex Way Rosé, letting the burst of citrus cleanse her palate before responding.

"This place I'm staying rents Airstreams. Can you believe this is a thing now?" He pondered this while she continued. "It's fully furnished, and they manage everything. And actually, it's pretty cool. I feel so vintage and Marie Kondo at the same time." She laughed, letting the bubbles surface as she swirled her glass.

"It's all about simplifying," he said. "My ex-wife got really into this phase of minimalism that I embraced. Less clutter, more focus on what matters."

She nodded. "Yes, my separation has made this a reality, whether I like it or not. He gets the house, pool, and Jacuzzi, while I am living out of my suitcase and what I have in a storage locker." She grinned and then corrected herself. "It's not as bad as it sounds! It's made me realize how much junk I have accumulated. And the freedom I have to go wherever I want is priceless."

Zach considered this as he took another taste of his deep red. "What is it about us that makes us need to accumulate things? I wonder if this comes out of our parents' and grandparents' generations recovering from the wars, Depression—"

"The dust bowl years," Kate added.

"Yes. They were making up for the fact that they literally had nothing. So, once they could afford to, they tipped the scales dramatically in the opposite direction."

"My parents taught me the importance of having material things," Kate agreed. "I mean, we don't need all these gadgets, but somehow it makes us feel like we are richer. More meaningful?"

He nodded. "I think it's also a matter of

control and security. Overcoming the fear of losing again."

She took another sip of her rosé. Looking at him across the table, she watched a bright orange butterfly flit by between them and then followed as it paused on top of the stone wall, resting its delicate wings. Turning back to him, she said one word, "Fear."

He looked at her, waiting for more, while she fingered the bottom of her glass, turning it ever so slightly on top of the wooden barrel. "How much of our lives are just about managing our fear?" she said.

His eyes lit up knowingly. "Oh, absolutely. I think fear is the main driving factor for many people. It doesn't matter how many advanced degrees we have, how much knowledge we have accumulated, or how much money we have. We still have this humming current of fear just under the surface."

"Yes, but that doesn't keep us from trying

to control it, right?" He nodded in agreement. She continued, "We buy all the things we are told, live the life we are expected to, accumulate the wealth, and yet we are still unfulfilled. We're still wondering when we will lose it all." She turned toward him, smiling a bit impishly, "Sometimes the best cure is to lose it all right, Doc?"

He winked at her. "That's certainly one way to realize that no matter what, you will be okay. This fear of losing everything is just an emotion. The reality is that we can recover from the worst. Just look at our grandparents."

Kate smiled with the memory of her beloved World War Two veteran grandpa. "I really do think they were the greatest generation. I still can't imagine how he fought all the way through the Battle of the Bulge and liberated one of the first concentration camps." She shook her head sadly. "The stories he finally shared near the end of his life were just horrific. Yet he came home as a loving and happy man. He honestly is still one of my best role models in terms of facing trauma and carrying on. Of course, that generation was not all touchy-feely. They didn't share their emotions openly, as we do now."

Zach agreed, "Oh, heck, no. My grandfather was a very tight-lipped, toe-the-line kind of figure. He just didn't believe there was anything we couldn't do. And he could not stand weakness."

Kate's eyes lit up. "Ooh, there's something; the idea of weakness and how we try to remove that vulnerability, and show false bravery, which is really just a flip side of fear." She finished her glass and set it down. "I mean, aren't all you men messed up with this idea that you can never be anything less than valiant, brave, and save all us damsels in distress?"

He grinned and winked at her. "Isn't that what you want? I thought I was here to rescue you from a horrible wine tasting experience!"

She grinned and brought the back of her palm to her forehead dramatically. "Oh, thank you, good sir, I just don't know what I would have done without your expertise. Truly, you have saved me from myself," she said in her best imitation of Scarlett O'Hara.

They sat back for a moment, letting the sounds of their voices fade, replaced by the chirping of birds and the wind rustling through the dry oak leaves. She heard a car horn beep in the parking lot beyond the courtyard, and then let her eyes rest on the peacefulness of the moment. She loved that they didn't have to talk all the time and that their silences were just as full as their conversation. She felt all glowy, warm, and content. In fact, she realized she hadn't thought about her novel or her soon-to-be ex-husband in hours. Usually she would hear a battery of critical voices playing in her head throughout the day. Instead she just heard her own breath as she took a deep one and let it out blissfully.

They finished their tasting and he turned toward her. "Are you ready to grab a bite to eat somewhere?"

She looked at her watch and realized it was only 4:00 p.m. All her senses were overwhelmed and she was ready for quiet time with herself. "No. Actually, I think I'll head back to the park and see if I can make any progress writing my plot line."

"Totally understand." They walked back toward his car and climbed in effortlessly. As he turned on the ignition, he asked, "We are still on for tomorrow's trip to explore downtown Fredericksburg, right?"

She breathed in the closeness of him and in that moment felt the urge to bridge the distance to kiss him. Blinking, she nodded, "Yes, yes." Adjusting herself back into her seat to fasten her seat belt, she said, "I'm really looking forward to that."

His eyes lingered for a moment on hers before he turned his attention to his rearview mirror and pulled back out of the parking lot.

After he dropped her at her car, Kate fumbled for a bit with her keys and then slid inside her SUV. She took a deep, nervous breath and let it out. *Phew*, she thought, *what a day*. Maybe it was the wine, but all her thoughts just turned into one blanket emotion of . . . happiness? Could that be? She laughed at herself and turned on her ignition to settle in for the windy drive back to the park. Is it possible to fall for a man in twenty-four hours? She shook off that thought and remembered that this was only a week, and she certainly couldn't expect anything more. Somewhat sobered by that thought, she instead chose to ride the bubbly wave of attraction and let those warm thoughts carry her back to the trailer.

———

KATE WOKE UP AND felt a damp chill in the air. She rolled out of her cozy bunk in the camper and padded her way down the short hallway to the kitchen sink. Filling the coffeemaker, she rubbed her eyes and regarded the detritus from the evening before. Empty cheese wrappers, a plate with an uneaten piece of dry salami, and pistachio shells littered her counter. Kate remembered having a wonderful picnic, listening to music, and dancing around the trailer before promptly passing out by 7:00 p.m.

She grabbed her favorite coffee mug and settled into the leather dinette seat. Through the aluminum-framed windows, she could see that a thick fog had settled in overnight, with soft grays padding in between the spaces of every tree branch and structure at the park. She felt instantly comforted after all the bright sunshine and heat. This was like a humid hug.

She shivered inside her sweater and took a

long sip of delicious warmth. French roast. *Oh, what would I ever do without coffee?* she thought as she smiled and basked in the afterglow. Kate's mind flitted back and forth through the images and bits and pieces of conversation from the day before. She could hardly believe that she and Zach would be meeting again in a matter of hours. Was that just a dream?

Just then, her phone began to vibrate on the counter, and as she reached for the phone, she saw her screen light up with "Caroline." She answered warmly, "Howdy! Greetings from Texas!"

She heard her friend's friendly voice on the other end of the line. "Well, howdy to you too! And it's about time you answered. I was wondering whether I needed to send out a search and rescue unit."

Kate giggled. "Yes, well, I was a bit distracted yesterday." She continued to share with her friend all the details of the delicious day with Zach.

"Well, girl, I can't say I'm surprised," Caroline said. "You always have a way of drumming up magic wherever you go. It's one of the reasons I'm your friend, so I can live vicariously through your stories."

"Well, you locked down the most amazing bachelor and have two beautiful children. I have to make up for it somehow!" She laughed. "I mean, I know this won't lead anywhere, but at least it's taking my mind off my deadline. Plus, you would totally love him."

"I'm sure I would, darling. Just don't forget you *do* have a deadline."

Kate smiled at her light scolding. "Yes, Mother. I gotta go and get ready. Today Dr. Wine is meeting me downtown, where hopefully I can do a little shopping as well!"

They said their loving good-byes and hung

up. Kate connected her iPhone back to the charger and stood up, taking a nice long stretch and touching her fingertips to the camper ceiling. *Here we go*, she thought, *day two of the unknown.* With that, she headed toward the back of the silver capsule to begin getting ready. All the while she was humming from a song by Louis Armstrong that surfaced from the night before, "Give me a kiss to build a dream on . . ."

⇛   Six   ⇚

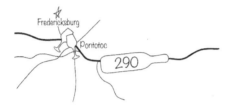

Fredericksburg

Pontotoc

290

D owntown Fredericksburg was a hustle and
bustle of people meandering to and fro. Decorated for the holidays, the streetlamps boasted
festive green and red wreaths just waiting for
nightfall to shine their twinkling lights. Settled
by German families in the mid-1800s, the in-
fluence of that culture could still be felt in the
architecture and food. The wide street spanned
eight blocks overflowing with boutique stores,
galleries, wineries, breweries, restaurants, and
other delights. Beer gardens were interspersed

on the strip, and restaurants boasted bratwurst and other traditional German fare. The sidewalks were dotted with tourists ambling along, peeking into store windows and pointing out places across the street to visit. Kate could only imagine how busy it would be over the weekend. She saw the brake lights flash on a black SUV and quickly stopped behind to grab a lucky parking spot in front of the quaint storefronts.

Kate decided to arrive a little early so she could wander through the boutiques. She loved getting lost in shops almost as much as she loved finding a small, locally owned bookstore to spend hours searching the stacks for that perfect timely read. She stepped up onto the cracked sidewalk and maneuvered around a red wood post to begin poking in and out of stores at her leisure.

She spied a row of beautiful handcrafted nutcrackers lining a storefront window and had the urge to buy one to decorate the trailer, but then decided against it. This was just her temporary home, and she didn't want to grow too attached.

Farther along, a hat shop's display opened out onto the sidewalk, and she realized what she needed most was a good straw hat to shield her fair skin from the relentless Texas sun. She tried on a few and checked out how she looked in the small mirrors hanging from the window openings. Finally she settled on a wide-brimmed one that fit snugly but comfortably and sported a thin striped white and black band around its base. Settling her bill, she continued on with the boost of adrenaline from her purchase.

Then she ducked into another boutique, which had the cutest southwestern designs in the storefront window. She made her way through the store, peeking between the racks at "Cowgirl Up" bedazzled shirts, and faux cow fur lined purses. Dangling turquoise earrings were displayed on an island in the center, and she held up a pair to see how they would offset her long, pale locks.

"Those look gorgeous on you!" the store-keeper said while straightening a stack of over-sized cardigans.

Kate smiled back a bit self-consciously. "Thanks. I'm not used to wearing anything so large." She paused and then shrugged. "When in Texas, I guess?"

The woman smiled at her. "Absolutely, girl! Bigger is better!" And with that she turned to help another customer as Kate placed the ear-rings back on the table and contemplated the purchase. *Why not?* she thought. *Maybe it's time for me to show off a little.* She had spent the past few years fading into the shadows of her hus-band's light. He didn't like her getting too much attention, and she was trying to do everything to make the marriage work. She figured that was just part of being married, that it wasn't all about her anymore, and that she needed to play the part of a supportive spouse. She found over time that she kept giving more and more of herself away in the process, and it still was never enough.

Today, looking back at the earrings, they reminded her of the old Kate. The Kate who was fearless and fiery. The one who would laugh loud, dance in the street, and howl at the moon. She missed that Kate. Picking the pair back up, she felt the weight in her hands, and the way they sparkled big and bright put a smile on her face. *Today is the day I bring back that Kate.* She headed toward the register, and on the way impulsively grabbed a matching wide silver and turquoise bracelet. Yes and yes.

She stepped out onto the sidewalk with the earrings dangling against her long neck underneath her wide-brimmed hat. Smiling, she felt a new spring in her step. If she was going to wear these, she needed to *wear* them.

Off she strutted, taller and with more

confidence. She noticed a few appreciative nods from passersby and felt that it was time she owned more of the space she inhabited instead of giving it away. Humming along with each new step, she caught a glimpse of herself in one of the storefront windows, and for the first time in a long while, she liked what she saw.

A pecan Danish and coffee later, Kate had about thirty more minutes before she was due to meet with Zach. The thought of seeing him again made her insides giddy with excitement. Bits and pieces of their conversation had sprinkled through her thoughts all morning. Images of how he held his wineglass. His long, tapered fingers. His ruggedly handsome smile. The sparkle in his eyes when she said something he liked. The easy way they were together. She still couldn't believe that this had happened.

A nagging voice immediately interrupted her thoughts. *You have a deadline and you'd better start to figure out what to write, missy!* Somehow her inner voice had taken on a southern accent. Kate laughed at herself as she justified that today's adventures could be chalked up to research, and shrugged the doubts away as she stopped at a selection of cowboy boots displayed in a wide window. She had always wanted a pair, but they seemed a bit impractical for everyday wear. Glancing between the beautiful options in red, turquoise, black, and white, she saw a row of ankle-high brown boots, and her heart skipped a beat. She had been eyeing these in magazines and had seen a few being worn around town. They were like half of a cowboy boot but without the stiff, tall part. In brushed brown leather, they zipped up at the heel and would look perfect with the skinny jeans she had on today. She rushed inside the store to see if they had her size.

As she stood at the floor-length mirror, Kate felt like Texas royalty. The boots hugged her feet and gave her just a hint of height, but with comfort. They seemed to make her legs longer, if that was possible. Maybe it was just the angle of the mirror, but Kate didn't care. She loved her new look: the hat, earrings, and boots set off her soft white V-neck shirt, and she felt like she was finally dressed the part of the cowgirl she'd always wished she could be. To Kate, Texas women exuded confidence, style, class, and a whole lot of spunk! That's something she was missing in herself, and something she desperately needed an injection of.

She put one hand on her hip, and the other she faked holding a gun and fired a bull's-eye at her image in the mirror and then laughed to herself. She then saw a clock on the wall. *Shoot, gotta scoot.* She hurried back down the sidewalk to stow the evidence of her purchases in the backseat of her SUV. *Let him think this is what I look like all the time.* She touched up her lips with some tinted gloss and then spun around to hurry back up the sidewalk, humming, "These boots are made for walking . . ." as her new boots led the way.

Kate had just arrived at the courtyard entrance to Pontotoc Vineyard when she caught sight of the back of his neck. Zach was a bit taller than Kate, and his dark brown hair was neatly trimmed short just above where the white collar of his shirt lay against the base of his tanned neck. *God, he really is gorgeous*, she thought as she watched him turn around, scanning the tables for her. She waved her arm, flashing a smile, and she saw him smile back in relief.

"I wasn't sure if you were already here, but figured not, since they still had wine to taste," he teased, and gave her a quick wink.

She blushed slightly as she teased back, "Well, it's a good thing you weren't one minute later!"

They openly smiled at each other, seeming to pick right back up where they left off just hours before.

"This building is one of the oldest in Fredericksburg," Zach stated as he guided her along large stepping- stones to a spot in the corner of the walled-in yard. Kate looked appreciatively at the limestone building, with the worn old beams of wood framing the single-paned windows. A tall, ancient palm stuck out from behind a pecan tree, its trunk wrapped with dry, gray fronds. They stepped around a raised firepit that was burning some mesquite, where a couple sat deep in quiet whispers as the cackle of the fire caught the chilled air.

Once they settled into their spot, Kate looked up at the red lit "Weingarten" sign hanging from the side of the building. She immediately felt cozy and comfortable. The waitress brought them both Mason jar glasses filled with a bright red concoction.

"This is our house specialty, sangria. Made from our grapes here in the Hill Country. Enjoy!"

She walked away as Zach turned to Kate

and raised his glass. "You look fantastic! Those earrings are SO you!"

She held up her palm, cupping the bottom of one. "What, these old things?" Laughing, she flipped her head dramatically and added, "I couldn't help it. I think I realize now what I've been missing my whole life: Texas bling."

He nodded enthusiastically. "Well, they totally suit you. And the hat looks great too."

"Honestly, I had to step up my game being around you. What with your tailored shirts and all . . ." She trailed off, smirking at him over the top of her glass and enjoying the tingling sensation as the cold liquid met her tongue. *If every day were like this, it would be like Christmas.*

"So let's see, where were we?" He noodled her thoughts and she breathed into the moment.

"Pretty sure we were solving the world's problems," Kate replied with a cock of her hat and a wink.

Their laughter met easily. Then they settled

back into their seats to discover their surroundings. Looking around the yard, Kate regarded
the holiday decorations suspended from the
tree branches above.

"Do you like the holidays?" she asked him
and then took another chilled sip.

"I used to quite a bit," he said. "Growing
up, holidays were so full of color, anticipation,
food, friends, and family. We would all pile into
the back of this Econovan—me and my brother
and sister—and head up to Tulsa, where my
grandparents had a small homestead. We loved
it. The family all together, traveling in the cozy
van, my folks not bickering, and everyone in
a festive mood. They had the meanest turkey,
which would chase us around the yard." He
started laughing and Kate smiled, watching his
face relax with joy. "What about you?"

"Well, we weren't as close with our extended family as we had hoped." Kate took a moment to think about how she could describe the

intricacies of her family dynamics. "My holidays generally consisted of me spending time with my mother and sister, Lillie. We would always have this huge fourteen-foot tree, and I loved to sneak out late at night after they were asleep to sit in the glow of it. I would pretend I was Clara from the *Nutcracker Suite* and dream of my prince as I would curl up and fall asleep underneath the canopy of tree branches." She smiled softly as she remembered the sharp freshness of pine and the twinkle of the lights peeking around the handmade ornaments, creating a halo of color and wonder.

"Really, the best thing was that I would get a stack of books every year that I could read through the break. It sounds totally nerdy, but I loved reading. It was my way to escape the reality of a sometimes difficult childhood. I would completely lose myself in the characters. In the hurts, the misunderstandings, the joy, the love." She stopped, then added, "Hope. Those were the stories I loved the most, the ones that gave me hope that there was a better world, a better time somewhere in the future."

Zach took every word in and just let her have that moment. Kate surprised herself that she had opened up that much, that she had shared such a vulnerable moment of her past. Even more so, she was surprised that she was completely comfortable with it. Perhaps just the fact that he wasn't trying to fix her past, or interject his own opinion, was enough for her to realize she could have her own memories and feelings without needing to defend herself or explain. He simply accepted her for who she was.

Breaking the nostalgia, Kate added, "This is actually my first Cactus Christmas. I grew up in Port Angeles, Washington. We didn't get snow every winter, but it was blustery and cold, perfect to bundle up by the fire and embrace the season. This is a totally different experience."

"Really? That's beautiful country," he said.

"I tell you, I actually am happy to be down here and getting a break from the cold and snow back in the Northeast. This. This is how people should spend the winter: T-shirts, sunshine, and wine."

"Tell me about your sister, Lillie?" he asked as he took another slow sip.

"My sister, Lillie . . ." Kate paused as she fingered the stem of the glass.

How could she explain the difficult dynamics of her relationship with her sister? She felt protective of her and somewhat abandoned by her.

"Lillie is a really talented singer/songwriter currently touring in France with her band. We don't talk much anymore, but I think she's happy doing what she loves."

"I'm sorry to hear that you aren't in touch with her. Sounds like a fascinating life, though," Zach said, letting the moment be still.

"You?" Kate returned.

"My brother and sister are older"—he winked at her—"but I take pride in being the only one unplanned." He laughed at his own joke and broke the tension. "I was the big surprise that got all the attention." He grinned at her. "They live near Waco and we try to visit as often as we can. Another reason I'd like to spend more time down here in Texas."

They both finished their glasses so they could move on, to the next place. Kate was reluctant to leave their quiet sunny patch tucked away from the frantic noise of Main Street. She followed Zach back through the entrance, marked by an old German-style carved wooden gate.

The atmosphere of the place jogged Kate's inner love for the holidays. A memory deep within from her childhood that had been buried. She hadn't felt like celebrating since her mother had passed away over the Christmas holiday a few years ago now. She and Lillie had come together in the Pacific Northwest for the bittersweet ending. Then Lillie immediately embarked "on tour" to France.

Kate was left to attend to all the details herself. She couldn't really be angry with Lillie; Lillie was much younger and had been dealing with the brunt of the care up to the end while Kate was on the South Carolina coast. But she did feel the absolute loss of so many things in that single instant. The loss of family. The loss of the season. She felt that Christmas would never again be special. Strangely, her ex-husband didn't much like the holiday either, so it was easy to avoid the decorating and merriment each year. Instead, she attended only the obligatory parties, but tried to forget the season as much as possible. Yet there was part of her that still held hope.

As she walked next to Zach along the sidewalk, nodding at the other tourists, she thought about how this season could be different. Maybe it was time to stop avoiding the hustle and bustle, and find unexpected joy in the magic of it all?

Zach nodded to a family across the street all dressed up in matching red and green knit caps and laughing together. "Of course, my daughter loves celebrating the holidays."

Kate regarded the small, closely knit family with a tinge of envy. How she wished at times she had that security. Knowing that she was part of a unit. Needed. She heard him continue, "It's one of the reasons I've stuck around the Northeast after the divorce. Being able to share the holidays together was important for me. Even if just for a short time, I'm grateful that my wife and I can look past our own issues and just enjoy our amazing daughter that we produced together."

Kate had more questions, but just then he nodded to a doorway up ahead. "Here 'tis. Our next stop: Fredericksburg Winery."

Zach opened the glass doors, and Kate

stepped through into a large, open room. The building itself gave off the appearance on the outside of a strip mall. Once inside, Kate saw the rows of bottles proudly displaying medals. The space was sectioned off with wooden shelves filled with goods, and the whole feeling was very unpretentious and approachable. They moved to the long wooden bar at the back of the room, where Zach did the honors of picking out a few selections to taste.

He turned to face Kate. "I know this place may not have all the charm, but they have a huge heart and are one of the top producers in the region."

"Do they grow their own grapes?"

"Actually, they purchase grapes from some of the other vineyards in the region—Bingham, Bogar-Cox, Diamonte Doble, Newsom, and Pheasant Ridge, to name a few. I know this because my buddy from school, his family is connected to the Newsom family by marriage.

They started with just a few acres of Cabernet grapes and now have more than a hundred and fifty." He looked at Kate with a glint in his eye. "Their story is the reason I think it's possible to get into this business if you have the right land and family . . . or partners." He handed her a glass with a lighter shade of red.

She took a taste of the F&N Zinfandel, noting the subtle sweetness as the delicate notes washed down her throat.

Leaning against the bar, Kate picked up on the previous thread. "Family. I often wonder what I've missed out on not having kids myself." She wasn't sure why, but she felt like she could be open and honest with Zach in a way she couldn't with her own friends and family. "I think there is something about having kids, knowing you are living on in some way through them. That you are creating a legacy . . . I think maybe that's the part I really wonder about. That once I'm gone . . . well, that's it?" She shook her head suddenly. "I'm sorry if that sounds incredibly melancholy."

Looking up into Zach's eyes, she saw kindness and compassion. "Not at all. I often wonder what my life would be like without my daughter. I mean, it would be a lot less expensive and quieter." He laughed softly. "But although she seems like the greatest thing I've produced in this life, I also know that there is so much more I can contribute."

She pondered this. "I guess in a way I always considered my writing to be my baby. I give it life, nurture it, tend to it over time, and then release it into the world, hoping for its success." She smiled a little and then added, "It's still expensive, of course."

"You know life isn't all about ticking off those boxes," he said. "I mean, it's great that some people can find early the right person they can love for years, and have beautiful children, and manage their life and careers. Yet it rarely turns out like we think it will. I think if you trust and pay attention, life has a way of managing itself."

He presented her with another tasting, this time Baron's Bach Burgundy, before continuing, "I had this patient once who thought he had done everything right. He had lived up to his parents' expectations, following into their line of restaurants. He built up the business and had quite a positive reputation. Married his high school sweetheart, had three beautiful children. He worked every day and late nights to provide for them. His wife stayed home with the kids to home-school them. He had it all planned out, that he would be able to pass on the responsibilities to his eldest, and continue the legacy his father had begun. Then he began having health issues. He ignored them and continued to push himself feverishly, figuring he'd have all the time he needed. He kept losing weight, didn't sleep, and couldn't eat. He figured it was the stress of the business, that he needed to be stronger and less weak. So he pushed even harder.

"When he finally came to me he was in so much pain he could hardly stand it. The tests came back and he had pancreatic cancer. He passed away within three months." Zach looked at Kate very solemnly. "You see, even when we have everything we need, we still want more. If he had listened to his body and taken care of himself, getting tested early and changing his lifestyle, he could have had more time to spend with his kids."

"That's so sad, and so true," Kate said. "It seems like we are always looking at the other side of the fence and thinking it's greener. Or trying to live someone else's life, thinking it will make us happier."

"So maybe kids weren't in the cards for you personally." Zach looked right at her with soft eyes and an open heart. "I know that you are meant to be doing something amazing with your work and that you will touch lives in a way that far exceeds what you would accomplish raising a family."

Kate's eyes began to fill with hot tears as she swallowed hard and let herself just stay in the comforting moment between them. "Thank you" was all she could push out. She was pierced to her core as his words went right to the root of her pain and sadness and melted them away in an instant. "You have no idea how it feels to have that kind of reassurance. Having to decide not to have children was one of the hardest things for me. I think partly because I longed for that family myself and partly because biologically I felt the need to fulfill that duty." She shrugged at him as she dug through her purse for a tissue. "I know that the reality is that even having children doesn't mean you will always have them."

"Hell, if there's anything I've learned in my

years of practice is that life has its own agenda," Zach said. "We can plot and plan all we want, but when our number is up, that's it. The advice I give all my patients, and myself if I'm listening, is this: live your life fully in each moment. Don't wait for what you think tomorrow will bring, and don't waste time regretting the past. The cliché is true—life is incredibly short, and it's meant for us to fully live, grow, experience, and share."

Kate felt the deep waves of emotion begin to recede within her as she rested in the comfort of this moment with him. This moment at a wine room in the Hill Country of Texas. She had absolutely no idea what her life would be like in the future. She had no plan. Just a book needing to be born and a compass to set her direction by.

She said, "You know, you really do have an amazing bedside manner. I bet you are an incredible doctor."

He blushed a bit and sat back. "Well, I have amazing patients, and I just do my best to be as human as possible."

They finished up and walked back to his car to head to the next winery, a bit farther away. Kate settled into a moment of quiet as she heard the snap of the car tires on the gravel as they pulled onto the paved highway. She let the purr of the engine fill the space between them, pondering the intensity of the moment they just had.

⇒ Seven ⇐

He pulled into the white graveled parking lot of Lost Draw Cellars, and turned off the ignition before smiling back at her. "Ready?"

Any awkwardness from the previous emotions had evaporated on the short drive away from downtown as Kate responded, "You bet."

They stepped out and walked past a low fence to find a seat in the open courtyard. The sun was fully overhead and shining brightly now, and they found a spot underneath one of the red and green patio umbrellas. The winery was pretty busy, with a wedding party taking up one side of the beautifully terraced patio. The black metal tables and chairs were arranged comfortably, and Kate could hear the sounds of water gurgling over rocks from a water feature opposite the covered patio. A pianist was playing and singing softly as the conversation rose and swelled gently in the early afternoon breeze. "Chestnuts roasting on an open fire. Jack Frost nipping at your nose . . ."

Kate laughed to herself as she realized there was no way she would get away from the season. Fredericksburg was prime for it.

As they received their first tasting of 2018 Reserve Roussanne, they listened as the host explained the malolactic fermentation process. Kate took a sip and distinctly noticed the creamy texture and taste of the red. They nodded to each other in agreement as they sipped quietly, taking in the flavors and the scenery.

She was thinking about the different twists

and turns in her life and how she was now sitting here enjoying this moment in time. It was as though all of those crazy bends in her path were suddenly starting to make sense. She finally broke the silence.

"How many of the choices in life are predetermined versus choices we can make ourselves?" She trailed off for a bit before adding, "I guess what I'm trying to say is, how much of our life is up to us to dictate? How much control do we really have?"

He smiled and nodded as he chewed on that morsel of truth. "Honestly, I think we focus on the wrong things. We try to control the things we can't and we don't bother controlling the things we can."

Kate's eyes lit up. "Yes! Tell me more," she prodded.

"For instance, how many of us focus on trying to control outcomes with other people?" he continued. "I mean, we try to manipulate situations in our relationships rather than see and accept each other for who we really are."

"That's so true. I think that it's so much easier to focus on what other people are doing, and to judge them, than it is to truly see ourselves. Isn't that why we need relationships in the first place, to be our mirrors in a way?"

"Oh, yes. That's why they are so difficult. To find someone who will reflect your true self back to you without manipulating the image. Without judgment. To just be."

Kate pondered this as she thought about her own difficult marriage. "I think the hardest part about this is that the people who know you the best, the people whom you open up to the most, are often the ones who hurt you the deepest. How do you maintain a level of openness with someone and also protect yourself?" She raised her glass to her lips to take a slow sip, this time a 2018 Mourvèdre.

He regarded her thoughtfully as he recalled

his own situation. "When we first were married, we wanted to know everything about each other, and of course living with anyone for any number of years, you will know them better and more intimately than anyone else. I think that was fine at first because we were working toward the same life goals. We were both invested in creating this life and family that everyone expected us to, and we truly believed that it would bring us happiness."

He swirled his wine around in his glass thoughtfully. "But I think where it got tricky is when we started growing. When we started changing within ourselves and discovering differences between us that soon became insurmountable."

"Yes. I think if both partners are invested in growing and learning together . . . of having an almost childlike view of the world, then they are able to more easily navigate the life changes we all go through getting older. The phases

of growth and death, if that makes sense?"
Kate said.

"Absolutely. I mean, it's no mystery that we are all headed to death eventually, some sooner than others. It's a matter of our choices and decisions between here and there."

She agreed. "It all goes back to what we are basing our decisions and choices on. I mean, I think many of us base our decisions on duty or expectation. But are we really happy? How do we reconcile choosing our own happiness if that means someone else may not be happy with our decisions?"

He laughed. "And that's the precise reason why many people never venture down that path at all. They are content to coast along and let others decide for them and ride the waves of disappointment and bitterness instead. It's not living."

"What is your definition of living?"

He gestured around him. "This, for one!" They both laughed.

"Seriously, I think that to truly grow and live, you have to make difficult decisions. Unless you are willing to risk your ego's need to be in control and safe, and press on into the unknown, you will never truly know yourself.

"We aren't meant to be happy all the time because we would never appreciate it properly. I know this is sort of cheesy, but it's like the seasons: there is a reason for those cycles of life, death, and renewal. And who are we to think we are above it all? I think we do our best to trick ourselves into believing that life is about controlling every outcome, when life is actually about understanding our true place in the world."

"Interesting." Kate pondered before adding, "And that place is very fluid. I mean, when I am embracing the 'flow' of life, I am a much happier person than when I am projecting an outcome that never measures up."

"Exactly."

Kate took a taste of the bolder 2018 Tempranillo. "So if this theory is true, then why is it so hard for us to embrace this as a culture?

"We spend all our time reinforcing this belief that change is bad and that staying the same is good."

He nodded with a sad look on his face. "Wouldn't it be so great if everyone celebrated the changes and growth over years rather than just clocking years? I mean, that's how my marriage began to feel—how many years have we logged versus how happy we are. Like that milestone of twenty-five or fifty years together makes up for the fact that we could be incredibly miserable the whole time. Don't get me wrong, I believe that marriages can last that long and be happy. Yet I think most of our relationships start off on the wrong foundation, and certainly many become very toxic and unhealthy. We shouldn't place more importance on time over quality."

"Amen," Kate said emphatically. Then she added quickly, "But, of course, we do hope they will last. That is the dream, right?"

Zach shook his head emphatically over the wineglass. "Of course. It is a tragedy when you invest so much time and energy into something only to have it not work out."

They both thought for a moment, and Zach swirled his glass slowly around, displacing the liquid gently, and then spoke.

"I think my ideal relationship is one that truly ebbs and flows with all the changes in the tides. Maybe sometimes we grow or change at different rates, but we are committed to loving each other through it and give each other the freedom to explore and discover on our own."

She stopped to look at him squarely. "You know, my girlfriend Caroline told me, 'Just because you are married doesn't mean you stop being yourself.'"

"The best marriages I have seen involve some level of compromise for sure, but they are based on the understanding that each partner respects the other as an individual," he immediately replied.

"It takes two sides to make one coin," Kate said as they both felt that truth.

They both took a sip on that note and let the enormity of the conversation rest between them.

As they finished their tasting, Kate wondered if she would ever find that partner. Not perfect, but just right. It seemed that her whole life this search proved futile, and if there was a golden egg out there she had yet to find it.

Zach took the wheel, and Kate nestled comfortably into the passenger seat again as they headed east on 290. She marveled at their easy rhythm. She also wondered at how different it would be without him there. He said he was leaving at the end of the week. Kate had no plans to head to the Northeast, and well, it was just plain complicated. She had just left complicated, and was paying a very high price. She took a deep breath and let her eyes rest on the blooming cactus and clumps of dried grass as they drove the short distance out of town. She could handle this. She was an adult, after all. Besides, she reasoned to herself as she watched him reach for the dial to adjust his seat, she was still in control. He was a perfect gentleman, and probably not even interested in her anyway.

She knew that she had a long road of healing in front of her. Timing was everything. But it was really nice to just enjoy these moments right now. She didn't have to pretend to be anyone else. She didn't have to try and woo him. She simply had to be herself. Zach was someone to hang out with and discuss random things over delicious glasses of wine. Honestly, it was a perfect situation.

Wasn't it?

She looked back over to him and her eyes followed the barely perceptible stubble beginning to form at his jawline. *Damn*, she thought, *why am I always attracted to the ones I can't have?*

He turned to her in that moment and a mischievous grin broke out, changing the contours of his face. "Penny for your thoughts?"

She laughed and blushed slightly, turning back to look through the passenger window. "Oh, I'm just thinking about how much you are going to miss when you leave." In that moment, she could have smacked herself in the forehead. *What in the world, Kate?* She realized that perhaps the last tasting had taken away that filter normally in place that would have caught her from making a fool of herself. "I mean, you know," she added lamely, "this countryside is so different from the Northeast." She cleared her throat trying to cover up.

He looked back to the road, and then at her

again with a glint in his eyes. "Yes, I will definitely miss the beautiful scenery." He smiled at her fully before turning his attention back to the road. Kate could feel the warmth inside her as she took in that compliment and let the glow spread throughout her chest.

The glow of hope.

He flipped the blinker on and they waited for some traffic to pass before turning off the highway and into the parking lot.

Their final tasting of the day was at a smaller, unassuming wooden building, Los Pinos Ranch Vineyards.

They started by tasting the featured wine, a Texican 2018. The deep red looked enticing as they made their way to stand around a wine barrel away from the bar and just in front of rows and rows of beautiful bottles of wine resting on open racks.

As they took a sip, Kate noticed the spicy smoothness at the end of the dry red.

"So tell me about your writing," Zach said. "Did you always want to be a writer?"

Kate finished her sip and let the raspberry notes tingle her palate. "Yes. Well, I mean, I didn't always know, but I always wrote." She looked at him impishly. "I actually first wanted to be a ballet dancer." His eyebrows rose as he waited for her to continue. "Yup. I would take class at the dance studio three times a week, ballet, jazz, but mostly ballet. I would stand at the barre, struggling through the complicated exercises, trying to perfect my turnout underneath that poster of Baryshnikov with the torn tights and duct-taped shoes, and dreaming of someday performing professionally."

She laughed. "Of course, that dream included him falling in love with me and us dancing duets all over the world." Zack returned her laugh fully.

"I grew up and did dance all over the Midwest at least. I performed countless *Nutcrackers*, and even went to Europe to audition." Kate hummed the *Mirliton Suite* and sat up in her chair with her arms in a high V, her delicate fingers stretched out to the notes.

Zach seemed impressed. "So what happened?"

She let her arms fall and settled back into her chair unceremoniously. "Age. That's what happened. That and the fact that I wasn't blessed with the stick-thin slender body now all the rage."

"Wow. It really is a short life span, right? How old were you?"

Kate smiled ruefully. "Twenty-eight. I retired at twenty-eight with bad knees, bunions, and a slew of debt. I was actually barely eking out a living in New York City, and it was time for me to move on." She looked at him squarely. "But that was one of the most difficult transitions for me. You know, dance was my whole life up to that point. What was I going to do? Who would I be if I were no longer the"—she raised her fingers with air quotes—'dancer.'"

He nodded sympathetically. "Yes, that must be really tough. I mean, it sounds like you were living the life of an athlete, but with the pay of a starving artist."

"Exactly. I can perform all sorts of complicated combinations, tell you the proper way to turn out from your hips, and identify classical scores in just a few phrases. But where does that get me offstage? I had to find a different outlet for my creativity." She looked up with one eye and added, "And a really, really good therapist." They both laughed and took another sip of wine.

"So essentially you are in your second career?" Zach asked.

She smiled as she pondered the road from there to here and the twists and turns between. "Well, it wasn't exactly a straight line by any means. I mean, I went back to school to get my bachelor's later in life, and then just sort of cast about until I finally found something else I could be equally passionate about."

She laughed to herself when she remembered feverishly writing her first novel. "Actually, my first book came out of a bathroom-floor moment." She raised her eyes in a dramatic pause to catch his inquisitive look before continuing, "Yes. I had found myself facing bankruptcy, and unable to afford to continue living in New York. I was desperate, lonely, and feeling like a complete failure." She swallowed those feelings down before continuing, "I was drowning my sorrows with some friends at McSorley's one afternoon, trying to figure out what to do, when one of them told me about this writing workshop in the Berkshires. It was three months over the summer and had some of the best authors in residence to help curate and critique. So I applied and was awarded a work grant, where I would clean up the facilities at night to pay for my room and board." She smiled, remembering how determined she was. "It was backbreaking work, and I didn't sleep much, but I wrote and wrote. And finally I ended up with the first draft of my book, which was picked up by my agent."

"Wow, fantastic!" Zach toasted to her. She smiled triumphantly as she raised her glass to clink delicately against his.

"Yes. It's hard to believe that was just, what, seven years ago now." She pondered everything that had happened between now and then. How she had met her soon-to-be-ex-husband right after publishing and finishing her first book tour. "That time seemed so exciting and alive. I felt as though I was finally swimming in my lane and that the prize was in sight." She shrugged. "I mean, I was riding on this wave of adrenaline and excitement, and then I met my husband and it just seemed to be this magnificent crescendo. Too bad the wave had to come crashing down."

He nodded to her, listening intently the entire time.

"I'm sorry," she said quickly, blushing as she realized she had been talking for far too long about herself.

"Not at all," Zach said. "I am absolutely fascinated. It's such a different life than the one I have lived. I mean, there is no set path, just a lot of hard work, hope, and luck."

She nodded. "Timing is everything."

"Time. It never seems like there is enough, is there?" Zach said with measure. "It always seems like there will be more time. Time to get better. To reach that next level. To get that job. But then you realize all too soon that your time is up."

She chewed on her lip. "I knew it would go quickly, but I truly had no idea how fast. I had no idea how lost I would feel after. Dance was my first love, and I suppose it always will be. Do you know, I still dream about it?" She laughed to herself.

"It's been twenty years, and I still dream

that I am onstage or in the studio rehearsing. Those dreams used to haunt me. But now I delight in them because I know I could never be that limber again in my life."

"What an amazing life you have led so far," he said.

"Well, it certainly sounds much more glamorous than it was at the time."

Zach laughed. "It always does. That's the power of the story. Speaking of, tell me about what you are writing now."

Kate raised her hands, laughing. "Fact or fiction?" She shrugged and emptied her glass of wine. "I am writing my first fiction novel, and trying to blend some truth with the overall story, but I keep getting stuck. I know I have to pull together my draft and I'm hoping that if I drink enough wine I will have a magic epiphany. So if some of our conversations make it into my characters' dialogue, please excuse me. I have to find inspiration wherever I can."

"Absolutely. Anything I can do to fan the flames of inspiration and art," he agreed.

They laughed and he looked at his watch, and she realized how late it had gotten as well. "I suppose it's time to quit for today?"

"Yes, I have some calls I need to make tonight, so I'd better get you back to your car," Zach said as he got up and held her chair out for her as she stood.

"Such a gentleman." She smirked and felt for a moment dizzy in his closeness. "Thanks for listening to my sad stories."

"No, you are amazing, Kate." He looked at her squarely and said, "I mean that." She opened her mouth but couldn't find anything to say back. She felt vulnerable and safe at the same time.

He led the way out of the tasting room as the white 290 shuttle van unloaded a group of passengers at the entryway. They were festive and loudly chatting back and forth, and Kate felt for the first time that she wasn't missing anything, that she was right where she needed to be. Her mind and heart were full. If anything, just the past few days were an incredible gift to her. As they walked outside, the twinkling lights wrapped around the trees began to shine brighter as the sun was dropping behind the building.

Wonder. That one word was all she could use to describe the feeling she had right now. The magnitude of this moment. The wonder of the season.

They pulled out onto the highway as the blinking Christmas lights gave way to the intermittent headlights of cars whizzing past, a string of red brake lights ahead in the distance. She felt as though they were two beautiful ornaments strung along this moving tree of life.

⇗ Eight ⇐

Kate was still floating high on the wine and conversation and was sliding her key into the Airstream door when her phone buzzed angrily from inside her bag. She stepped inside, closed the door swiftly behind her with a bang, and dug through until she found the small device and pulled it out. She saw missed calls and a stack of green bubble text messages that expanded once she unlocked the screen. Immediately she was brought crashing down to earth as she saw the commanding message from her soon-to-be ex-husband.

"Call me."

Kate swallowed all of her emotions and reluctantly dialed his number back. It was still fairly early in the evening and she imagined he was likely outside at their pool drinking a mojito or entertaining one of his many friends. How seductive that lifestyle was to her, and how quickly it became a trap.

"Hello," he answered with a fatherly disapproval in his voice. "So nice of you to finally make time for me in your busy life."

Kate grimaced and had to prevent herself from slipping into old patterns when she would apologize and explain and try to make him feel better. "What do you need, David?"

He cleared his throat. "Obviously, what I need is a wife who isn't afraid of being loved and who will come back home instead of running away."

Ouch. Kate had to be one of the most openly loving women, and to be criticized for that
played right into her own need to be loved in
return. How could he turn the tables so quickly
in his favor?

"I didn't run away, David. I left. There is a
difference," Kate said.

"Marriage is a commitment that you work
out. You don't just leave."

Kate thought how this marriage wasn't what
she signed up for. That she had wanted a true
partnership, not a lousy contract. And what
about his role in all of this? Instead, she kept
silent knowing it would only end up in more
circular arguments that she would lose.

"You still have some of your things here." He
said the word "things" as though it were dirty
and a nuisance.

"Can't you keep them until this is finalized?
I made sure to put everything in the attic so
that they aren't even there for you to see." She

begged somewhat, considering she didn't have anywhere to put the items and no way to retrieve them easily.

Kate had brought everything she could carry herself when she first left. Unfortunately, there were a few family keepsakes she couldn't manage by herself. She had hoped to have more time to return to retrieve them later to take to her storage unit, but as soon as he heard from his "staff" that she had packed things up, he had all the locks changed.

"No. You need to get them now." Any trace of charm or love was now gone. He sounded like a stranger. She was the problem. "You have until the fifteenth, and then I'm calling junk removal."

Kate swallowed her anger. Of course her things were junk. It didn't matter that these were all of her own belongings she had carried with her over the past forty years. It didn't matter that he would be destroying the 1950s wicker furniture from her grandparents that she had received after their passing.

"You know I don't have a way to come get my things so quickly, and I don't have a place to put them," Kate pleaded.

"Whatever. You have the deadline. You made this choice. Everyone thinks that I'm being too nice by not getting rid of it already."

Kate's blood pressure began to rise, and she refused to let him get the better of her. "Fine. I have to go." She hung up as he was asking her, "When? When will you come?"

Fuming, she knew there was no way she would ever see her things again. She couldn't risk being near him. He would turn on the charm and try to convince her to stay. If she didn't comply, she knew he would call the sheriff's department and say she was harassing him and trespassing, and likely be able to get away with it as his nephew worked there and would have his back no matter what. Hell, after hearing his version of things, that she had abandoned him for no reason, she knew there would be many people ready to give her a dose of revenge on his behalf.

No. Sadly, she left with only what she could take in her car. She had to make yet another sacrifice to save herself.

She looked out the window of the trailer at the twinkling lights wrapped around a pecan tree and marveled at how quickly her holiday cheer had turned sour.

She tried to shake it off, and instead focused on tidying up her living quarters and doing the dishes by hand. She was washing a mug with a green cactus on it when she felt herself slipping back into that familiar depression. He could hit her right where it hurt, and somehow she still believed him on some level. Maybe she was unable to love? Maybe she wasn't meant to ever be in a good relationship?

She set the mug down on the draining rack

and turned around to lean against the sink as tears began to fall down her cheeks. It didn't matter how much she loved or tried. Here she was alone again.

She began the downward spiral of mental beration. What was she thinking, anyway? Here she was, traipsing around town with some handsome stranger, behaving like she could escape her reality. She wasn't sure she could write a good novel. She had failed in her marriage. She was renting a trailer with no idea where she would go after the holidays. She was the loser.

Kate let the big tears flow down her face as she slid to the floor and collapsed in a heap. All her bravado gone, she just let her body rack with sobs. The loss of hope. No kids. No marriage. No family. She felt in that moment the enormity of her pain. Even as mean as he was, just hearing David's voice reminded her of the man she once loved so fervently.

Kate continued to shake and roll on the floor

until finally no more tears would come. She opened her eyes and took a shallow breath. Looking at her laptop and the stack of papers, she realized that she couldn't continue whatever this was with Zach.

She had to protect herself. She would have to cancel their plans for the rest of the week and face the reality of her deadline. Without that novel selling, she would be completely destitute. She had to finish it.

She sat up slowly and wiped her eyes, steeling herself as much as she could manage. She didn't have time to play around with some guy who wouldn't care about her one whit after this week. She didn't have time to avoid her responsibilities any longer. It was time she grew up. *Forget love, missy. You need money and stability. You need to make your own future. Don't trust anyone else.*

She felt the stubborn pride in her rise, and she picked herself off the floor. What kind of a grown woman would spend her evening crying over a jerk? It was time she faced the facts. Maybe she wasn't lucky in love, but she had to use the one thing she was good at: writing.

She dismissed the voice in her head that began saying, *Yeah, but your last one didn't do too well. Are you sure you aren't just wasting your time? You could go back to him and be taken care of again . . .*

No. Shut up.

"I can do this," she said out loud in the trailer. Then she said it even louder, and over and over, "I CAN DO THIS!"

She punched her fist in the air, working herself into a frenzy. Forget men! She would write, and write, and she would prove David and everyone else wrong.

She threw herself into the dinette bench and opened up her laptop and just began to type. It didn't matter anymore what she typed. She just needed the rhythm and the cadence to remind her of who she was and what was important to her.

This was her livelihood. Hell, this was her salvation.

The blue light of the screen reflected off the trailer window as Kate focused all of her energy on the pages before her. Off in the distance, she could hear coyotes begin to call, and she felt like joining them.

⇉ Nine ⇇

The next day came a little too early for Kate. She groaned to herself as her eyes felt puffy and her soul bruised after last night's reckoning. She did finally get her plot and characters mapped out, but her heart wasn't 100 percent into it. She struggled out of bed and began to make coffee. The cabin of the trailer was nice and cozy, and the sunlight streaming through the windows did a good job of hiding any darkness from the night before.

Her phone buzzed on the counter and she flipped it over to see a photo of Caroline lighting up the screen.

"Hello, friend," Kate answered flatly.

"Oh, wow. You sound completely pathetic. I thought you were on a high with your wine prince, or Dr. Wine, or whatever you call him," Caroline prodded her.

Kate pushed the aero press plunger into the coffee cup—today's choice was a ridiculous cartoon Rudolph with googly eyes. "Ugh, yeah. Let's just say that the past has reared its ugly head and last night was a doozy."

She could hear Caroline sigh before answering. "Oh, darling. I'm sorry. What's going on? I've been worried about you being all alone. I know this season isn't the best for you. Are you okay?"

Kate poured cream into her cup and then took a long sip before answering. She felt the warmth of the coffee and her friend, and she savored that feeling. "Oh, Car . . . it's like I can't get past my past, you know? It seems like every time I try to change direction, move on, get over things, I am right back where I started."

"Is this about David? Or just life in general?"

Kate laughed a little. "I guess both. I mean, I just don't know what I'm doing anymore, or why." She paused to swallow as her throat tightened with grief.

Caroline continued listening as Kate poured out all of her feelings to her good friend. She didn't have to explain or defend herself because Caroline had her back from moment one.

"I think the hardest thing is for my mind to accept reality. I mean, I really thought marrying David was going to be this total dream come true. I was so absolutely infatuated with him. Here I was with someone already accomplished and with such a fascinating public life I was sure we would be a dynamic couple taking on the film scene and that my writing would just be an extension of this. I thought I would no longer be alone. That I would finally have that one person, that partner who would have my back. Whom I could grow old with and rely on. But that partner turned out to be so self-involved and cruel."

Kate let the sentence drop as she thought about all of the machinations she had gone through trying to make the marriage work. Everything she did was criticized. Her bangs. Her makeup. Her past. David made a point to stick his finger into every area of her life to take control, calling it love.

Caroline cut into her thoughts. "Yeah, but you didn't know that when it started, Kate. You went into this with the best of intentions, and honestly I'm surprised you lasted as long as you did."

Kate laughed ironically. "If lasting three years is long, I may as well give up altogether.

"The thing that bothers me the most is that

although I know how horrible it was and how much I had to leave, I still feel that my side of the story will never be heard."

It wasn't Kate's style to sling mud back. That didn't mean she was lacking for any reasons or proof; she just preferred to take the high road over continuing to stay in the arena, where she would only get more deeply entrenched in the lies, insults, and shame.

She brought herself back to the present and asked Caroline softly, "So when will I finally be able to move on? If I did the right thing for me. Why do I feel like he's still winning?"

She added after a long pause, "Why do I still miss him?"

"Oh, darling, he will always win. He is the big fat ego in the room who needs to be right all the time. You were never going to win, and you were never going to be happy. And of course you miss him. He was your absolute world for the past five years," Caroline consoled her.

"The best thing you can do is look to your future. I mean, you have the chance to write the book of your dreams without any distractions from him or his world. That alone is a blessing. You'll see, time is a wonderful healer."

Kate sighed to herself and prayed internally, *A blessing is exactly what I need.*

She agreed with her friend. There was absolutely no way she was able to write well with him around, and a big reason why her second book flopped. She hadn't fully put herself into it. It was like she had cashed in all her chips on her marriage, and she was bankrupt.

Caroline prodded her further, "Hey, so how is the writing going? Are you making any progress? And what is happening with your wine guy?"

"I finally mapped out a plot line and characters last night. I still feel like I'm forcing myself, though. It's just not coming easily. I think I've lost my confidence in . . . everything," Kate admitted sadly. "Zach has been amazing. Our conversations have made me remember what I missed in a good relationship, and the wineries have been so much fun to visit."

Kate perked up a bit at the thought of him. "Honestly, I don't know if I should continue, though. I mean, he's totally out of my league, and he's only here this week. I feel like I'm starting to like him just a little too much." She sighed into the phone to Caroline. "Will I ever find my true prince?"

"Absol-freakin-lutely, gurl," Caroline said with her low-country drawl. "God is just cooking someone up for you special, and he's just not ready yet. Kate, you deserve to have an amazing life and partner. Don't even question that for a minute. It's up to you how you want your future to be. You can either keep beating yourself up for the past, or you can take all those lessons you've learned and move forward. The choice is yours."

Kate nodded in agreement. "Besides," Caroline added, "it's not like David's waiting around. He's already moved on, you know?"

Ouch! That hurt, but Kate knew it was true. He was already dating his "friends" and continuing to live his same lifestyle, just without her. "How can someone I only knew for a few years have such an incredible impact on my life?"

"Well, honey, that's love, I'm afraid. Whether it's good or bad, you still get sucker punched at some point in time," Caroline said. "Which is why you just have to enjoy the ride." She added, "In the meantime, you have Dr. Wine as a temporary stand-in."

Kate laughed ruefully and chatted for a bit longer before hanging up with her friend.

She looked at her laptop, and then out the small metal windows of the Airstream to the world outside. Kate thought about what her friend had said to her and took it to heart.

Why should she sacrifice happiness now? Would her guilt and hurt fix anything?

Nope.

Kate sat down and let her gaze rest on her folded hands. *God, forgive me, but I'm going to grab my happiness where I see it—as long as I'm not hurting anyone.*

She heard a loud pecking noise and looked up to see the most beautiful bright red cardinal fluttering and pecking at her through the reflection in a window. She laughed and took it as a sign. One hardhead to another. She understood in that instant that giving up wasn't a choice.

This was the sign Kate needed. A new year. A new novel. A new perspective on her life and future. Instead of beating her own head against a window, she should be celebrating the fact that she saved herself. She pulled herself out of the wreckage and now her future was wide open. She was only responsible for herself, and she was doing a much better job of making those tough decisions. They all added up to her new vision of her life. For the first time in a long while, Kate was proud of herself. She wasn't selfish. She was full of a new appreciation of her own character and sense of worth. And she was done being manipulated into giving herself away to anyone else.

She would have to get over any nagging tinges of guilt that she felt from the past and instead embrace the luck that had been placed on her path leading to her future. Maybe Zach was a unicorn, but at the very least, he reminded her that they exist. And she wasn't quite ready to let go of his good luck charm just yet.

⇒ Ten ⇐

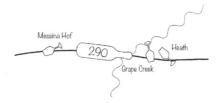

Kate pulled into the beautifully manicured parking lot of Messina Hof Winery. The building was magnificent, reminiscent of a French country chalet, with a stone-laid round tower in front giving the feeling of a small castle. The grounds were immaculate, and when she stepped inside, she felt as though they were stepping back in time. A beautiful, simpler time when the only thing they had to do was sip wine and converse. It felt exquisite.

Any doubts Kate may have had about seeing

Zach again vanished in his warm smile. She felt immediately comforted and exhilarated. He ushered her to a table he had already chosen and she sat down to enjoy the first tasting of the day.

"I took the liberty of making a departure from our red flights and instead thought we would try out their Rieslings," Zach said, proudly holding up the tasting card so she could see that the flight was titled: "Give me one good Riesling."

"Perfect," Kate said. "I'll take two!" They laughed together, and she already felt bubbly and warm before the wine even arrived.

"I have been thinking all night about your life," Zach said, taking Kate by surprise.

"Really?"

"Yes. The fact that you have already lived such a full life, and how brave you are to continue to try new things." Kate felt herself blushing and hid her nose in the wineglass until she recovered. "You are such an inspiration. I wish my daughter could meet you. I feel like she's struggling with her own identity right now and she could use a positive role model."

Kate raised her eyebrow and said, "Well, I really appreciate that. I've never felt like a role model for anyone. Tell me about her."

Zach settled into his seat and got this far-away, sweet look on his face as he thought about his daughter. "Chloe," he said softly, smiling. "She is such a beautiful girl. Smart. Talented. But she's struggling with being a teenager right now. Unfortunately, that means she's not too happy with her mother, and is testing her boundaries left and right."

Kate nodded, remembering her own teen-age years and how focusing on dance was her saving grace. "Does she have hobbies? Sports?"

He smiled. "She loves to read. In fact, that's all she wanted for Christmas—a big stack of books that she could read over the break."

Kate laughed. "Well, I think Chloe and I would get along just fine."

He nodded in agreement before adding, "Her mother would like her to be more socially active. Her mother is part of the country club set and was in a sorority in college. Her feeling is that Chloe will never meet her future husband if she doesn't join more groups and put herself out there."

Kate gasped. "Wow! Preparing for a future husband at such a young age?"

"My ex-wife is part of a family steeped in history and entrenched in the local architectural scene," Zach said. "There are a lot of rules and expectations, one being that Chloe is expected to find a suitor within the appropriate society circles."

Kate grimaced. "What do *you* want for her?"

He shrugged, taking a moment to swirl his wine around the glass slowly. "I just want my girl to be happy and to know she can become anything she chooses. She is the world to me, and I am not too fond of how people in my wife's circles treat one another. Mostly I can stay out of it because of my practice and the hours. But I have always had a difficult time fitting in. All that focus on money, family tradition, and entitlement." His face scrunched up like he had tasted something sour. "It honestly turned me off, and is a big reason why I wanted out."

Kate nodded in support. "Well, the thing is once Chloe goes to college, a lot can change for her."

"Indeed. And for me too," he replied, as if he were trying to tell Kate something.

"I've actually been encouraging her to apply at my alma mater, UT. My ex-wife will kill me, but I think the best thing for Chloe is to give her the opportunity to be more independent and to find other friends more on her level intellectually. And I won't lie that it would align with my dreams of relocating here as well." Zach took the last sip of his wine and set down the glass.

Kate pondered his remarks as she finished,

just in time for the host to bring the next selection.

"I have an idea for you," Kate said after taking a sip and letting the warm notes wash over her tongue. "You should get Chloe a special journal. She's at such a great age of self-discovery, and I bet encouraging her to write down her dreams, passions, and desires will help her to channel some of that teenage angst in a positive way."

Zach nodded thoughtfully as he considered this possibility. "Yes, I could see that. She's at that age when it's difficult to find something personal to give to her, and I really do want to encourage her creativity."

"I started journaling when I was her age," Kate said. "Sometimes it was like a diary, sometimes I made up fictional stories and characters. I would scavenge through all the magazines in the house and cut out pictures of people and places that made me happy. You know, like a beautiful snowy cabin in the mountains, or a white farmhouse kitchen, or pictures of nature and the open road. I totally wanted to do a road trip by myself across the country." Her eyes sparkled as he watched her reminisce. "I just imagined the adventures I would have, the people I would meet, and places I would see— oh! I know! You should get her a camera!" Kate bubbled over enthusiastically.

"Actually, she is really getting into photography and has a fantastically curated Instagram account."

"Of course she does." They both laughed. "Yes, but I think the idea of teaching her the art of photography could go hand in hand with the journaling. Help her to visually tell her own stories," Kate said.

"Now you're talking." They toasted glasses and took another sip, settling into quiet as they let the words between them float down.

They watched other couples come in and

let the soothing sounds of conversation and the clinking of wine- glasses fill the space between them as they finished their own tasting.

Stepping back out into the bright sunlight, Kate was appreciative of how vulnerable Zach had been. She wasn't the only one to share her feelings, and that made her all the more comfortable with him. She trusted him. She laughed to herself at this, because it had been a while since she had felt that level of intimacy. Trust was so important. She looked at him as he unlocked his car door and she thought how it always started out this way. Is it possible that it could stay? That this level of innocent intimacy could remain over years? She settled into the leather seat and let that idea float around while he started the ignition and they headed to their next destination.

Just a short distance farther east on 290 she saw a stone sign beckoning them to enter the site for both Grape Creek Winery and Heath

Sparkling Wines. Kate reveled in the experience as they pulled up past rows and rows of
beautifully organized grape vines seeming to
go on forever. "How can we go from a French
chalet to what feels like Tuscany?" she asked
Zach, breathless from the wine, his closeness,
and the setting.

He smiled at her as he slowly made their way
up the gravel drive to the main property. "Isn't
it magnificent? It's a taste of the Old World right
here in Texas." She smiled back at him as he
pulled into a spot next to a granite black Tesla.

Kate wondered what his life was really like
back in Massachusetts. What did he drive?
Where did he go? What restaurants did he visit?
Then she quickly admonished herself. *Kate, you
had better not start really liking this guy because
you will just be in for a world of hurt, missy!* There
went her inner sassy-southern voice again.

She stepped out of the SUV and they walked
toward the entrance, taking in the beauty of

the expansive views. She could hear grackles chattering up a storm in a nearby oak as a hawk swooped gracefully overhead. Letting out a deep breath, she began to feel in that moment the tug of her heart never to leave this place.

"I did go to Italy on an audition trip when I was younger," Kate said out loud, sort of to herself. "But I never got a chance to see Tuscany or the wine country. Someday I will get there."

"Of course you will. In the meantime, this is a pretty good substitute." Zach opened the large front door for her. "Let's pretend we are there now, shall we, Doña Bella?"

She couldn't help swooning a bit, brushing past him as he theatrically gestured for her to enter through the arched stone doorway. *Good grief*, she thought. *Why on earth is he so darn lovely?*

Feeling the effects of the flight of fruity Rieslings, she agreed in the moment to believe in everything that was good. Adjusting her eyes from the bright sun outside, she took in the beauty of the room and entered a state of splendor.

Precisely laid stone-tiled floors, off-white stucco walls, and wrought iron chandeliers hung from the beautifully stained oak beam vaulted ceilings. Every finish was impeccable, and Kate was overcome with the romance of the place. Zach guided her to a floating bar that was exquisite with wooden scrollwork and a bold black marble top. She caught her breath as she felt somewhat dizzy from the experience. Wine bottles with medals were displayed above the bar, and crystal wineglasses hung in rows by their stems, waiting for the next moment to shine.

"I scheduled a private tasting if that's okay?" he asked Kate.

"Absolutely," she said as she motioned around her enthusiastically. "I can't wait to try their wines!"

He smiled and they followed their host to a private room with floor-to-ceiling glass walls overlooking the numerous rows of vines beyond. Dark wood, black trim, crystal chandeliers, and stonework. The contrasts were striking, and Kate thought she could live in a place like this. Forever.

They were guided through tasting some of the winery's finest selections, and then left to enjoy the experience in private. "I honestly feel like a million bucks," Kate said to Zach. "I absolutely love this design style; it feels comfortable and luxurious at the same time."

Zach nodded. "Yes, I think this is one of my favorite wineries. And although the Tudor style is beautiful, there is something quite breathtaking about the earthy Tuscan boldness."

Kate nodded while sipping her glass of 2018 Captivating. The delightful layers of fruit played on her tongue until she caught the buttery hints of caramel and butterscotch wrapped in a crisp oak finish. She couldn't tell whether it was the wine, or the ambience, or both. But she

could say with certainty that she was completely enamored.

"Tell me about your dream house," Kate
asked Zach suddenly as her eyes followed the
rows of Montepulciano vines to the horizon.

He shrugged a bit, then leaned back against
the thick wooden table as he pondered her
question. "I don't know if there's a specific architectural style I am drawn to. Definitely I
gravitate to midcentury modern clean lines and
that aesthetic. But I also really like the farmhouse or ranch style where it can truly be lived
in. And you?"

Kate smiled with ease as she closed her
eyes, thinking of her dream house. "Honestly,
it's more of a feel than a style. I have always
pictured this big table outside, with plenty of
seats for family members and friends. Bottles
of wine interspersed, and lots of really delicious food and laughter. A wide-open space
leading up to the partially covered veranda,

and a wraparound porch. Floor-to-ceiling windows and French doors opening up to let the evening breeze blow into the massive kitchen." She stopped and looked at him dead on. "It's all about the kitchen."

He laughed and agreed. "It's where all the action happens."

"I love style that inspires me with mixtures of nature and modernity. But I also think that a home should be well lived in. Like a beautifully loved, sandy, whitewashed beach house," she said, then added softly, "A place of respite. To be able to land and be protected from the storms of life."

Zach regarded her for a moment longer. She felt as though he was about to say something more, but then the host returned to deliver the next tasting of the flight.

They continued through the rest of the tasting, basking in the glow of the private room. Kate luxuriated in the view, and for a brief moment completely forgot her deadline and her ex. Zach was in a good mood as well, although he wasn't always easy to read. She wondered if she was overromanticizing their time together. Did he have feelings for her as well? She swallowed that thought along with the Sangiovese blend she was sipping, reminding herself that this was only one week and she shouldn't get her hopes up.

She watched the outline of Zach's frame from the corner of her eye. He was listening as their host was pointing through the glass walls toward the fields beyond. "Over there we have our Tannat and Petite Sirah grapes, and just beyond this field in front we have our newest field dedicated to Cabernet Sauvignon, Cabernet Franc, and Malbec." The two men chatted back and forth a bit about the growing cycles and region, the differences of the Hill Country grapes vs. the High Plains AVA. Kate just let it all fall into the background as she took a deep breath and let the sunlight warm her through the glass walls and the view soothe her soul.

She was lost in thought when Zach broke her concentration. "You look like you belong here."

She blushed slightly, wondering when their conversation had ended and how long he'd been looking at her. Smiling slowly, she turned to him, raising her glass. "Right back at you." They held the moment longer, and Kate could smell his familiar rugged scent as she peered into his deep blue eyes. Clearing her throat, she asked, "Are we ready for the next one?"

He smiled at her, seeming to enjoy her discomfort. "Yes. Let's go."

He turned away to put down his empty glass and she realized she had been holding her breath. Exhaling slowly, she set hers delicately next to his on the table and then followed him out toward the building next door.

Heath Sparkling Wines was a distinct departure from the Tuscan vibe. The modern

sharp-lined building was as crisp as the sparkling wine they bottled. Large windows vaulted
to the ceiling proudly displaying the angular
porch and vineyard views. Dark gray, white,
and cement. It was a striking minimalist palate
with sparse blue agave plants and white rocks
manicured inside white stone boxes. Inside, it
was open and bright. Kate felt like she had been
transported to Sonoma. In spite of the sharp
lines, the vibe was warm and like a clean slate.
Ripe with possibility.

They made their way to the long, angular
bar. Boxed islands with LED displays showed
bright views of the vineyard, cuvée, and fermentation method. Zach got the attention of
the gentleman behind the bar and ordered the
Sensory Fusion flight, sparkling wine paired
with culinary bites.

They moved away from the bar and decided
to sit outside on one of the plush white couches
overlooking the fields. Kate could hear the soft

gurgle of the water fountains out front. "The fresh air feels nice," she said as she wrapped her bright yellow pashmina scarf around her neck. She was comfortable, wearing faded denim jeans with her new boots and a cropped denim jacket over a white T-shirt. Her hair was pulled up into a loose ponytail and she chose minimal diamond-studded earrings that sparkled against her earlobes.

They sipped their first tasting, and the bright bubbles delighted her palate. A couple stood posing against the railing with their glasses raised as another woman took their picture with an iPhone.

The feeling was expectant, and Kate wondered if they were celebrating a marriage or anniversary as they beamed to each other and kissed quickly before turning around to take in the view.

She flashed back to the memories in her own history of champagne toasts and laughter among friends. It didn't matter how much she rationalized the situation, she still felt guilty for leaving. As though she alone could save the marriage. Perhaps she could have if she didn't mind losing herself in the process. No, she made her decision and was tired of having this back-and-forth argument with herself of should haves and what ifs. It was over. The decision made. She couldn't change who David was, and he didn't have any desire to meet her in the middle.

Zach reached out his glass to toast hers, and Kate looked at the bubbles popping and fizzing festively on top of the pale pink wine. She touched her glass to his and resolved to tuck away those inner thoughts as she raised the glass for a taste. This was not the time for an internal debate. This was a time to celebrate her future.

Just as they both were taking a sip, an older couple approached and motioned next to them. "Do you mind if we join you?"

Kate and Zach smiled and beckoned them to sit. "Absolutely, please do."

The man helped his wife get settled before sitting close beside her and then turning to them. "You know, we are celebrating our fiftieth anniversary. Can you imagine?" He beamed, the sunspots on his face lighting up as he looked back at his wife and she smiled warmly at them all. "Seems like just yesterday. Well, give or take a few years." She laughed and they all toasted their glasses and took a sip.

The woman had perfectly coiffed short blond hair curled from rollers and set so that they framed her face. She wore two long gold chains, and her fingers were adorned with various gold and ruby rings, in addition to her diamond wedding band, which sparkled in the sunlight and set off her French manicure. "Tell us, how long have you been together?" she asked Kate and Zach.

Kate began to blush and respond when Zach

interjected, "Five years now." Kate gulped down laughter as she looked at his sincere face. "We got a late start," he added, and they all enjoyed a good laugh.

Kate was relieved. She didn't want to try and explain their story, and any talk of separation or divorce seemed incongruous with the love and warmth of their celebratory moment.

"Tell us how you met," Kate asked them and took another sip of bubbly wine.

"Well, I chased her around for years before she finally agreed to marry me." The man's cloudy eyes laughed recalling the distant memory. "In fact, her own father said I couldn't afford her and to not even try."

With that the woman laughed and playfully slapped his forearm. "Oh, Earl. You know he was just kidding. You were always his favorite." She smiled at him dotingly, then turned to Kate and Zach. "Honestly, I think my father was just happy to get me off the farm and out of his hair."

"Now, it wasn't all peaches and roses," the woman said, "but we stuck through it."

Earl looked at her, lovingly patting her hand. "Yes we did, my dear Dorothy."

She smiled and then looked back at Kate and Zach. "And do you know what the secret was?"

They leaned closer for the revelation.

"Sex. That's the glue that keeps it all together." She laughed loudly, her whole face opening up, and Kate instantly loved her.

"Oh, for crying out loud, Dot," Earl said, but Kate could tell he was only playing embarrassed because then he added, "Well, we are now down to, let's see . . . once a day." He grinned like a schoolkid and they both laughed and leaned toward each other for a quick kiss.

Kate blushed, and she and Zach looked at each other at the same time in amazement. They laughed and Kate watched his laugh lines dance as he winked to her over his glass.

"Yes. I married the belle of the ball," Earl

added. "And let me tell you, this little lady here had many a suitor after her hand."

Dorothy rolled her eyes and laughed. "Oh, Earl."

"Don't 'Oh, Earl' me. I had to fight for you tooth and nail!" He laughed at his own joke. Then he said, looking at her, "Worth every second."

"Tell us about you. Where are you visiting from?" Dorothy asked before taking another sip from her wine flute. Kate looked expectantly to Zach and he took the bait.

"Well, we live in Austin now, but are considering buying land and building a house out here in the Hill Country." Zach looked at Kate to see if she would pick up the trail. She loved how his eyes danced when he was up to something. She figured, *Heck, I'm the fiction author, if I can't make up a story then I have no reason to write.*

"Yes, we met later in life, on a cruise ship, if you can believe that?" She patted Zach's hand lovingly before continuing. "He may not have been a champion at shuffleboard, but he sure made up for it in other ways." She trailed off suggestively and Dorothy winked at her with a conspiratorial laugh. "Atta girl!"

Kate could feel Zach's gaze on her and she purposefully kept her eyes locked on the woman so she wouldn't break her façade. "How about you? Where are y'all from?"

"Kansas. We are here visiting our daughter, who lives in Waco. We all decided to take the grandkids down here to celebrate the holidays, and then figured we would break away for our own little celebration." Earl nudged Dorothy.

"I sure hope we are as in love as you are when we are your age," Kate said. Zach nodded emphatically and then impulsively took Kate's hand.

She was overwhelmed in that instant with the love on display by the couple, and the warmth of his fingers against hers. *Oh, my gosh*, she thought. *What. In. The. World.* At this point

Kate couldn't string together a thought clearly because her entire brain and body were exploding with sparks.

Zach continued talking to the couple as though nothing were happening. "Yes, we are thinking of building a beautiful farmhouse with a wraparound porch so we can sit out under the beautiful Texas skies at night and watch the stars." Kate gulped as he began describing her dreams. Zach turned to her and smirked, then took his hand away to adjust his shirt collar. She immediately felt the absence of his warmth and longed for more. Kate wished in that moment that their story was true, that they were together and planning to live out the rest of their days in the Texas sun.

Earl pulled out a faded photo from his wallet and shared the photo with Kate. The edges were well worn from years of age, but Kate could see the image clearly. It was a younger Earl and Dorothy standing on what looked like a highway overpass. Earl was smiling and pulling Dorothy close while she was laughing into the camera. It was a perfect moment and completely captured their love to this day.

Kate handed it back. "What a beautiful picture. I can't believe you still have it after all these years."

Earl nodded as he put it back into his wallet and then looked at Dorothy. "And I still have my gal." They smiled at each other, and Dorothy patted his hand on her leg lovingly.

"We'd better get a move on, Earl. The kids will think we've finally run off." She smiled and turned toward Zach and Kate. "You two love birds keep at it. It's never easy, but boy, is it worth it." She winked at them as Earl stood up first to help her off the couch.

As they walked away slowly, leaning against each other for support, Kate wondered aloud to Zach, "Wow. Just when I think it's hopeless, something like that happens and makes me believe again." She could feel Zach nodding in agreement next to her. She turned to him and continued, "It's hard to be bitter and jaded when you see a love so pure. It also makes me wonder about how much time we waste."

"Absolutely." He looked at her softly, his eyes twinkling. "I'm sorry for being so forward earlier and holding your hand." Then he smiled a little naughtily. "I mean, I'm not sorry. But I didn't mean to put you on the spot like that. You were a good sport."

She gave him a playful punch on the upper arm. "I can't believe you lied to them!"

He laughed. "Well, if they believe us, maybe we are onto something?"

He shrugged at her impishly while she embraced that thought. Maybe she wasn't the only one feeling this chemistry after all?

They finished the last sips of their tasting, and Zach led the way out, toward the parking lot. "That's it for today," he said as he opened the door for her. Kate carefully maneuvered past him to slide into the seat, and he held her eyes for a moment before he closed the door gently.

Taking a deep breath as he walked around the back of the SUV, Kate let it out slowly. *Maybe, just maybe, her dreams would come true after all.*

They made their way back to Kate's car. He pulled in and cut the ignition, turning to her. "Kate. I know that this is a sort of delicate time, but I just want you to know that I'd never take advantage of you." She stared into his eyes, thinking, *I wish you would . . .*

"I know that. It's weird how I trust you after such a short time. I'm sure it's just your doctorly charm."

He winked at her. "Finally all that schooling paid off!"

She laughed and opened the door, stepping out, then leaned back in the frame. "I have really been enjoying this time with you. See you tomorrow." She waved and closed the door, watching as he gave a quick wave back and then started his car to pull away.

In that moment, Kate knew what she wanted more than anything. And there was the bitter realization that it would never work. She thought back to the couple earlier and desperately wished that she too could find someone to spend fifty years with. Heck, twenty would work too.

But the reality was that Kate had gone down one path into marriage, and now she would have to find her way back out again and weather the divorce. Alone. It wasn't time to be starting anything new with anyone. Besides, she didn't even know if Zach felt remotely the same. It was all wine-fueled speculation.

She started her engine and settled into the seat to drive back to the Airstream. When will it finally work?

She switched on the radio and pulled out onto 290 in the other direction. "My heart is

drenched in wine, you'll be on my mind forever . . ." Norah Jones and the steady rhythm
of the road rocked her gently as she made
her way home.

⇉ Eleven ⇇

Kate woke up that morning and stared at the shiny metal ceiling of her trailer. She didn't sleep well the night before, tossing and turning with dreams of missed connections and old loves. She felt as though she'd been running all night long, and was exhausted. Day four. She was sad at the prospect that she only had today and tomorrow with Zach before he flew back to his life in the Northeast.

She rolled over and threw her blankets off with exasperation. Trudging to the coffeemaker, she clicked it on and then grabbed her phone to text Caroline while the water heated.

"Hey you! Just checking in to be sure you haven't jumped off Jubilee Parkway. [laughing emoji] Text me when you can! [two heart emojis]"

She set it down and pondered her laptop, looking dejected on the dinette table. Ugh. I really, really need to get focused again. She then heard the "chewy, chewy, chewy" call of a Carolina wren and looked out the kitchen window at the oak tree wrapped with Christmas lights still lit from the night before. Christmas was just a month away. She had almost forgotten about it with all the distractions. Kate made a mental note to send another text to her sister.

Lillie.

How she wished they could someday be together again for the holidays.

Seven years younger than Kate, Lillie was an incredibly gifted musician. She was somewhere in France with her band, and the last Kate had heard from her was a few months ago for their usual check-in. With the age difference, they didn't have the same close bond that other siblings have. In fact, Kate left home early, at seventeen, while Lillie was still in grade school. More of a mother than a sister, Kate had always taken the role seriously. Even more so when their mother was diagnosed with breast cancer. Lillie resented Kate for that. She didn't need another mother, yet Kate didn't know how to show her love and give her independence at the same time. Their mother was their only tether. Once she passed, they just sort of drifted away to live their lives on separate islands. A sea of time in between.

Kate took a sip of her coffee and watched a bright red cardinal dart in and out among the tree branches. She made a mental note to try and bridge the distance the next time Lillie called. With her own island getting smaller,

Kate realized how very much she needed to rebuild the remains of the family she had left. She just wasn't quite sure how to do that without coming off as overbearing. Especially considering that this was the season of so much loss. She had to be delicate and let Lillie come back on her own terms.

She pulled out her phone and wrote,

"I hope your tour is going well and that you are eating far too much cheese and wine! Call when you can, I have some news. Bisous xxx K."

Oh, how she wished she had a family like Caroline's. A big, loud, overbearing family that would always gravitate home for the holidays with lots of laughter and cheer. Kate realized that sometimes you just don't get what you want. Instead of trying to create the family she always wanted, as she had hoped to have with David, she would just have to find contentment in her present reality. Perhaps she could live that dream life out in the characters of her novel? Maybe someday it would come true?

Kate let that thought percolate as she finished her cup, rinsing it out in the sink, and then pondered what she would wear today. Stepping to the back of the trailer, she rifled through her pile of clothes until she found a pale pink V-neck sweater. She pulled out a white button-up shirt and a pair of dark jeans, placing them on the bed. Perfect. She turned toward the bathroom and started the shower, waiting a moment for it to get warm. As she stepped into the narrow stall, her thoughts gravitated back to Zach. She wondered what kind of magic would be in store for them today. It seemed that every day this week she had experienced so many beautiful, poignant, and inspirational moments. She always wondered if they would run out of things to talk about, but they never did. Smiling at that thought, she lathered herself up and then let the sweat of the evening's tormented dreams wash down the drain.

Today's first winery, Ab Astris, was farther east on 290, closer to Hye, Texas. Latin for "of the stars," the winery was fairly new to the Hill Country scene. With a modest vineyard of a handful of acres, their pride are their Tannat grapes.

Kate was reading the review on her phone when she saw Zach pulling up the dirt road in the distance. She clicked her phone off and then stepped out of her car to meet him as he parked. He greeted her warmly. "You ready for today?"

"Wouldn't miss it." They fell into step and walked past big, beautiful live oaks standing proudly before the rows of grapes stretching out behind. "It honestly never gets old," Kate said, pointing to the view. "It's just absolutely beautiful to see all these vines day after day."

"Yes, this is a view I would never get tired of." They stepped inside the small but elegant tasting room and moved toward the bar. Zach was wearing a tan and blue crisp plaid button-up shirt underneath a dark blue vest with his sleeves folded partway up his muscular forearms. The vest met the waist of his ironed khaki tailored pants, and the folds left Kate's eyes lingering for just a moment too long.

"See something you like?" he teased her as she quickly held up the tasting sheet and pointed to the first wine she could, trying to divert him.

"This seems like a good choice to start," she lamely replied as she watched his laugh lines crinkle around his eyes.

"If I may say, you look beautiful today. That pink suits you well."

Kate thanked him and felt that flutter in her belly as they grabbed the stems of the tall wine-glasses and made their way outside to the patio.

Starting with the 2016 Cabernet Sauvignon, they swirled it around the glass before sniffing the hints of strawberry, spice, and rose.

Finishing the first taste, Kate let the blackberry and raspberry flavors slide down her throat before noticing the peppery finish.

They sat for a moment, watching a couple playing cornhole in the distance, and another sitting at a picnic table and talking close underneath a wide oak.

"Tell me something, Zach," Kate started. "I have been thinking about our friends from yesterday all night. I just keep wondering about how lucky they were to find each other so young and stay together so long."

Zach nodded, finishing his sip before placing his glass on the tabletop. "I know. I couldn't stop thinking about them either. What a pair."

Kate turned to him. "Do you think that love was just easier back then? Or do you think that we are just not patient enough now?"

Zach thought for a moment. "Well, I don't know if it was easier, but maybe they just didn't have the same options we have now." He let that idea float about before continuing, "I mean, we have all these ways to meet people: social media, travel, dating apps . . ."

"Perhaps less is more?" Kate said, raising an eyebrow.

"Exactly," he agreed.

Kate wondered about that for a bit longer before taking another sip of her wine. "Do you think our expectations are too high now? I mean, it's like we are all searching for the perfect person, which means we end up focusing more on each other's flaws."

"Yes, I wonder that too sometimes. But I also think maybe we understand ourselves a bit more as well. As a species we evolve, or we hope to, and the more we understand our own needs and desires and are able to communicate them, the more complicated relationships become in some ways."

"You think that being clearer about what you need would make things easier, but I guess maybe it just makes it more difficult to find true alignment with someone else," Kate said. "Like, for instance, in more primitive societies, the expectations for partnership were born out of survival: provide for each other, propagate the species, safety in numbers."

"Yes. And now many of those base needs are met already, so they become almost an afterthought. We have the time and resources to ask more questions and dig deeper into our own psyches. Ultimately, happiness is at a higher stake."

Kate nodded to him and looked back out over the fields.

"However, it's not always true that longevity equates to happiness," Kate heard him say as she took another sip of her wine. "I suppose it has more to do with what your overall outlook is, how you perceive the meaning of life."

"Ah, yes, the holy grail." Kate looked right at him and said matter-of-factly, "It's all about perception. If you think life is all about reaching one goal or destination and staying there, then you will place more emphasis on longevity and see unexpected experiences as detractors from your real purpose. But if you believe that life is a series of lessons and learning that you accumulate along the way, then you won't be as concerned with the numbers and the length of time, or even the goal at the end. Instead, your happiness will lie in the understanding of where you are at any point in time along the path." She watched as his eyes lit up in connection.

"Yes. It's all about the fixed or the growth mind-set."

"Which are you? Do you see success as reaching a certain goal? Or do you enjoy the journey along the way?" she asked.

"Well, honestly I've been both in my lifetime," Zach said. "I started off being very goal-oriented. A perfectionist by nature. Any deviation off the course was a failure. Then I started to realize I couldn't possibly control every outcome. Particularly when it came to my marriage." He looked back at Kate, sighing. "That's when I became really interested in embracing the growth mind-set. This idea that we can consistently grow and learn and fail forward. That is fascinating to me, and it seems a much more compassionate way to live." Kate watched as he stood and took the glasses back to the tasting room and returned with their next round.

Even after their interactions over the past three days, she was still fascinated at how he just totally got her. She was a pretty good conversationalist to begin with. Part of her role in her marriage with David was to entertain at his events. Yet so many times she would share her views and it just wouldn't click with the other person. They would absently nod or agree just to agree, but not really connect.

She took a sip of wine and thought that was

the rarest thing of all: the fact that they just always clicked.

The click factor.

He set her wineglass on the table and then settled back in his chair. "What about you? Have you always had a growth mind-set?"

She shook her head from side to side while smelling the cigar and cherry notes before sipping the 2017 Montepulciano. It was delightfully clean and velvety and she reveled in it for a moment before responding, "Oh, gosh, no." She swirled her wine a bit and then set her glass down. "Well, I call myself a recovering perfectionist, but I have always struggled against this idea of black and white, right and wrong. My mom came out of the fixed mind-set generation, so I had a very strict upbringing and a fair amount of guilt if things didn't turn out as she had planned."

Kate smirked at her memory. "Of course, that changed after she got sick. And I think she began to realize all the life she had missed trying to be 'right' all the time."

Kate shook her head sadly as Zach prompted her for an explanation. "Cancer. Breast cancer," she said flatly.

"I'm so sorry. How long since she passed?"

"Two years." She ruefully smiled, adding, "A few days before Christmas."

"Wow," Zach said, sitting farther back in his chair. "I'm so sorry. This must be a difficult time of year for you."

Kate shrugged a bit. "Honestly, yes and no. I mean, I loved my mother, but she was always a bit guarded— needing to do things herself. She kept everything a secret until she couldn't any longer. Then there was really nothing my sister or I could do. She went on her terms." She looked up at Zach. "I honestly just took it as a gift that she was finally at peace."

He gently met her gaze, speaking volumes without saying a word. She took another sip and redirected, "Anyway, I just think that is when I realized the importance of it all. Life is too short, and it really doesn't matter whether you are right or wrong, win or lose. It's all about the experiences along the way."

"Only you can live your life," he replied.

"Exactly."

Zach leaned back and motioned around him, "Like this, for instance," he said. "This week for me has been such a highlight." He looked at her warmly. "I honestly can't thank you enough. You've saved me from being alone with my own thoughts, and instead I've been able to truly enjoy this part of the country again."

He added, "I know that this is a tough time for you, but I also know that diamonds are created out of pressure. Your book is going to be the product of all this pain, loss, and soul-searching. It's going to shine."

Kate drank in his encouragement. It had been far too long that she had felt she had a champion on her side of the ring. She raised her glass, "Here's hoping you are right. And I am really glad we've met too. This week has been inspirational in so many ways."

They toasted, "To your book!" he said.

"To your winery!" she said as their glasses clinked.

Kate finished her glass and handed it over to him as he fetched the coveted 2017 Tannat tasting. Sunlight played through the leaves of the trees, and Kate felt the warmth of the wine spreading throughout her chest. It didn't matter whether he was "the one" or not. All that mattered is that she paid attention and stayed present for their last few days together. Then who knows? She shrugged off that thought with a shiver, instead reaching her arm out to grab the final glass from him.

They basked in the golden light on the patio while enjoying the silence of nature. Which wasn't silent at all, but instead a different kind of noise that took precedence as their words receded into the background.

The stillness reminded her of something her music teacher from grade school had said of the space between notes. That music would just be a wall of sound. It's the spaces that give it depth and beauty.

The space between them right now was that beautiful. Even and timely. Kate breathed the sharp, fresh air tinged with the muskiness of mesquite, cedar, and oak, and she breathed out, letting her entire body relax into that space.

At some point later, Zach moved and Kate realized that she had lost herself in somewhat of a trance. Satisfied, they left their empty glasses at the table and walked back to his SUV to head to the next destination.

Along the way, Zach stayed focused on the road while Kate gazed out the window. The trip was short, and they felt no need to fill in the silence yet. It was as though the moment were pregnant with all their thoughts and they weren't yet ready to push them out.

In minutes, they arrived at Hye Meadow Winery, a boutique winery with more than sixty acres of vines and a beautiful meadow of oak trees.

Zach pulled into a spot in front of a pair of unassuming midcentury modern buildings. He peered through the windshield as he pulled his key out of the ignition. "This place I am really excited about," he said. "My buddy was telling me about their fermentation process, and how they do a great job of taking their wines seriously, but not themselves."

She smiled at him. "Sounds like a perfect pairing."

They got out and walked together toward the glass doors of the tasting room. Once inside, Kate immediately loved the feel of the place. The room consisted mostly of a welcoming rectangular oak-topped bar that wrapped around, making it easy to take in the views from any spot. Glass sliding doors took up one wall and opened onto the patio with generous views of the acres of oak trees in the meadow. A strip of black paint wrapped around the room above the windows, where the current blends and tastings were written in chalk, including a very cute drawn snowman with "Happy Hye Christmas!" written in white and red.

"I love this vibe," Kate said as she leaned against the bar and scanned the tasting menu above. She could hear music coming from somewhere, a faint jazzy version of "Jingle Bell Hop." She nudged Zach. "Now this puts me into the holiday spirit!"

Turning back to her, he pointed above at the written menu. "They are known for their Mediterranean-based reds, particularly their Tempranillo." He handed her a glass of their first tasting, and Kate gladly took it. looking expectantly into the glass. "But to start, this is the 2019 Viognier. High Plains."

He lifted his glass for a sniff. Kate followed suit and immediately smelled honey and hints of sweet citrus. She sipped and then tasted the pear and apricot notes. "I don't normally like a sweeter wine, but this is delicious," she said as she took another taste.

They got to the reds and he suggested they continue the tasting outside. Kate nodded in agreement as she took hold of the 2018 Hye Jinx. "I love this name. Wild and playful!" She laughed and then followed Zach through the sliding doors out onto the covered patio.

Once outside, she located the source of the music. A trio was set up in the corner of the patio, and the singer was dressed in a red sequin shift dress and tall black cowboy boots while singing breathlessly, "It had to be you." Kate smiled; it had been a long time since she had heard live music, and she was reminded of Lillie.

There were a few tables scattered around the band, and they grabbed a couple of seats to settle in and listen. The guitarist plucked out the melody on his pearl white Gretsch, while the upright bass thunked out the bottom harmonies full and warm to the syncopation of the snare and high hat. It made Kate want to dance as she tapped her feet underneath the table.

The patio was strung with colored lights and lent an even more festive feel to the day. She leaned toward Zach. "Tell me, Doc. Do you dance?"

He laughed. "I've been known to cut a rug or two."

She raised her eyebrows "Oh, really? Hmm . . . let's just see about that."

She stood and pulled him to an open spot in front of the band. He immediately took the lead, grabbing her hands and twirling her away and to him, with perfect timing. Kate's laughter lifted over the notes as they shimmied and swayed together. She delighted at his coordination, and let herself be led around, not knowing exactly what move he'd try next. As the song reached the final notes, he spun her and then took her down for a dramatic dip, firmly supporting her back as she held onto his arm, arching her head back in glee. He pulled her back up and she came in close. Kate could feel his breath against hers as they stood still for a moment looking into each other's eyes.

The band transitioned into the next song, and the singer began, "At last . . ." They couldn't have timed it any better. Kate whispered, breathless from the exertion, "This is my favorite song."

Zach curled his fingers with hers, pulling her closer as he rested his cheek gently against her forehead. She wrapped her arms around his neck and they gently swayed against each other to the beautiful rhythm, completely and fully in tune with each other. "I found a dream that I could speak to . . ." Kate inhaled his scent, and it resonated with her deeply. A sweet, lingering musk. He held his cheek lightly to her forehead the entire time, and she could feel his warm breath against her hairline, making her shiver with longing. She resisted any temptation to pull away, and instead let herself stay in the moment. His chest pressed close to hers, their breaths in unison, the music surrounding them. She closed her eyes and could hear the festive sounds of the winery in the periphery.

As the song finished, he pulled away from her just slightly and looked down into her blue eyes. She felt like time stood still and wanted desperately to feel his lips on hers. Instead he took a deep, painful breath and released her, letting their arms fall until only their fingers interlaced.

"Let's take a break." He breathed through the

Heather Renée May

air thick with anticipation. Kate felt somewhat deflated as he held her hand and led her back to their table.

He settled her into her chair first, then pulled his closer so they could talk underneath the music.

"Kate." He sighed deeply and looked out over the meadow for a moment before turning back to her questioning gaze. "There is nothing more that I would like to do than to kiss you right now." Kate tingled with the knowledge that they both shared the same longing.

"But I know you are in a delicate situation, and I don't think it would be best for either of us." He reached for her hand to caress it gently. "Does that make sense?"

Kate looked down at his beautiful fingers as they traced her skin, giving her shivers. "Yes. No." She laughed and took her hand back to grab her glass of wine reflexively. She took a long swallow and then finally met his gaze again.

"I do. I know you are right." She laughed again to herself ruefully, her eyes glistening. "Oh, timing!"

Their eyes met as his laugh lines danced along the edges.

"Someday it might be right. But right now I have my daughter to consider."

"And I have a marriage to end and a novel to write." She finished his thought.

They both sighed together and sat back into their chairs as the music filled the space and they grew aware once again of their surroundings.

Kate was thoughtful for a moment and then asked, "Do you ever wonder how much of life is up to chance versus fate?"

"All the time."

She stared at the long stem of her wineglass, fingering its delicate length. "I often wonder what would have happened if I hadn't decided to marry David. It was all so sudden, and I felt the pressure that it was all or nothing. We either had to marry to continue, or I would lose him forever."

"You know, love shouldn't have those sorts of consequences, right?" he said softly.

"Yes, I do now. But at the time, I didn't. So I went down that path. In an instant, my life's trajectory changed forever." She pondered. "I don't regret the decision. I just wonder what my life would have been like if I hadn't said 'yes.'"

He took a deep breath and patted the back of her hand gently again. "You know, Kate, I believe things do happen for a reason. Even the bad things."

He let the weight of those words sink down for a bit before continuing, "Maybe your life would have been different, but I can guarantee we wouldn't be here right now. It's the experiences that bring us along this path. We can't second-guess our old choices with new wisdom. It just doesn't work that way."

Kate grimaced under the truth of his

statement. She knew over and over that she would have made the same choice. She knew that she deeply loved David and always would. Even if it ended up not being the right choice forever, it was the perfect choice for then.

Just then, a ringing came out of his vest pocket and he pulled away to retrieve his phone. "I'm so sorry, I need to take this," he said, and moved away from the table to walk toward the meadow. She felt the cold air where his warmth had been, and watched his back stiffen as he held the phone to his ear. He was nodding emphatically, and as he turned toward her she saw that his once relaxed face was now grim and taut.

Crap. She realized something horrible was happening, and wished desperately that she could stop it.

"Kate, I'm sorry, but I have to go." He looked at her. His eyes were dark.

"Chloe was in a car accident. She's at Mass General and in stable condition, but I need to go home immediately." Kate felt her stomach drop in that instant.

"Of course," she said. "Let's go." And she turned her head instinctively to grab her bag.

They rushed out to his car, and she could see worry lines on his face as she fastened her seat belt and he backed up with purpose.

Kate didn't quite know what to say, but the realization that their week had ended so suddenly made her feel dizzy. She tried not to think about the fact that this would be the last time they would see each other, and instead swallowed down that grief to focus on reassuring him.

"I can look online right now to see the next flight to Logan," she suggested as she pulled up her Chrome browser and searched.

"Thank you. It doesn't matter which airline."

She scrolled as he sped down the highway. "JetBlue has a direct flight getting in just after eleven p.m.," she said, and thought about how her time coordinating travel for her ex paid off in moments such as these.

"That's great. Do you mind reserving it for me?" He pulled out his wallet and handed her a credit card.

Kate nodded, automatically grabbing it. "Absolutely. You focus on the road." She felt a strange sensation of intimacy with him, that this would be what being married to him might feel like. And she realized in that moment how in sync they were even in a crisis.

"April 4, 1974," he said, and she laughed to herself that they were just a few months apart in age.

"Window or aisle?"

"Aisle."

She typed in his last name, Winsome. She punched in the numbers and confirmed the flight.

"Okay, you are all set." She handed him back his card, and he took it, thanking her profusely.

"I really appreciate you doing that for me. I just can't lose any time." He flicked on his blinker and pulled into the turn lane. After a series of trucks and cars went by, he turned left and pulled into the lot where her car was. She quickly unbelted from her seat and opened the door to hop out. He put the car in park and met her outside.

He put both of his arms firmly on her shoulders. "Kate, I don't want to leave you."

She took a shallow breath. "I know. It's too soon."

He pulled her close and held her for a meaningful moment before pulling away.

"Go!" She pushed him. "If we believe in all this predestined stuff, this is just a prelude." She forced a smile as he got into the Range Rover.

"I'll be watching for your book, Kate. You can do it."

Kate tried to memorize the lines on his face,

every part of him, taking a mental snapshot before it was too late.

"Hey! We'll always have Hye." She gave a halfhearted laugh and held his eyes for a moment longer before he closed the door and backed out of the lot.

And then he was gone.

⇉ Twelve ⇇

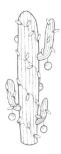

Kate stood there completely numb. His scent still lingered in the air, and it took her a moment before she could bring herself to step away and walk to her car.

She climbed inside and sat there dejected. *Well, what the hell now?* she thought as she just stared ahead at nothing. She looked at the passenger seat, and the wine trail map was poking out of her bag like a white flag. They hadn't gotten to visit the last winery of the day. Kate didn't feel like returning home just yet, so she resolved to continue. *Go hard or go home.* She stuck her key in the ignition and then backed up. She pointed the Durango east on 290 and drove forward, leaving the parking lot in a cloud of dust.

A few minutes later, she turned left onto a narrow road off the highway and made her way past more rows of vines and to the parking lot next to the tasting room of Ron Yates Winery.

Kate stepped out of her SUV and walked toward the ranch-style building. On one side a bar protruded out of the limestone from underneath a covered patio.

Beyond that, there were clusters of tables set out on a beautifully manicured lawn that butted against the open fields. Kate braced herself and stepped up to the bar, this time alone. She didn't have the heart to do a full tasting without Zach, so instead she chose a glass of the 2017 Mourvedre and found a spot by herself away from the crowd.

She took a long sip of the mixed blend, letting it coat her throat before exhaling a long sigh. Her phone buzzed with a text and she reached into her bag to grab it.

"How's Dr. Wine today? [wineglass emoji] xo."

Kate typed back one word, "Gone."

Her phone immediately lit up with Caroline's face and she swiped right to answer.

"What? Gone? What the hell? I thought you had one more day." Caroline demanded answers and Kate could hear the sounds of the road from the hands-free system. She took a deep breath before launching into the day's events. She could hardly believe the details herself as she shared them with her best friend.

"Okay, this story is horrible," Caroline stated disapprovingly. Kate laughed grimly in agreement. "I mean it, Kate. How the heck do you finally meet this perfect prince only to let him drive off into the sunset?"

Kate was silent, taking another long sip of her red.

"Go after him," Caroline insisted.

Kate shook her head. "Nope. It's just not the right timing."

"Timing schmiming," Caroline blurted.

Kate laughed at her friend "I have to believe as well. We met for a reason, and maybe it was just to give me the encouragement and push to finish my novel. I know it sounds cheesy, but if it's meant to be more, time will tell."

"I'm sorry, Kate. I really am. I know that someday things will work out for you," Caroline said lovingly into her ear.

"You know, I'm actually okay. I mean, I was in shock after the abruptness of it. Honestly, I am just so grateful it happened at all."

Kate smiled to herself and raised her glass to look through the clear top to the rows of vines beyond. "It's given me hope that magic really does happen. We just have to look for it." They wrapped up their conversation and Kate hung up.

She finished her glass of red and pulled out her orange notebook from her bag. Opening up to a blank page, she uncapped her pen and scribbled one word on the page: believe.

Placing it back into her bag, she walked to her SUV with a renewed sense of purpose. It was high time she got writing, and now she had a new focus for her novel. She would memorialize their time together. If there's one thing Kate knew well, it was finding magical moments in life. She would write a beautiful story to give hope to others. That it isn't too late. That it is possible.

Straightening herself a little higher, she looked out to the vines lying quietly in their rows and smiled, thinking. Someday.

She pulled onto the highway and headed back to the trailer when a few miles out she spied a small Christmas display on the side of the highway. She veered off the asphalt quickly and pulled over.

It's time to celebrate this season for myself, Kate thought. She was determined to make the best of the situation, and she stepped out to examine the metal decorations and wreaths stacked up until she saw the perfect little cactus peeking out underneath. It had little red Christmas balls and was wrapped with a single string of tinsel. Kate smiled to herself. *It's my Cactus Christmas: prickly and sweet.* She bought the little potted tree and put it securely in the back of her SUV before pulling out toward the RV park.

She smiled, thinking about Zach. His warmth. Their conversations. She knew better than to be bitter at the loss. Instead, she chose to embrace the unexpected gift that he truly was. Just when she had fully lost hope and thought she would never love again, he had appeared.

She rolled her eyes upward and said aloud, "I know you have a reason, and I'm just going to trust you on this." She smiled, looked back down at the road, and pressed her gas pedal to accelerate forward toward her trailer home.

⇉ Thirteen ⇇

With a week until Christmas, Kate put all of her focus into finishing her draft. Rising at 4:00 a.m., she crept through the quiet cabin to make her coffee and then nestled into the dinette bench, with a red plaid throw to keep her legs warm in the early morning chill. The park was still and peaceful, and Kate could hear the distant sounds of a train speeding across cold metal tracks. Not a creature was stirring, not even a mouse . . . She clacked away on her laptop keyboard, staring intently into the illuminated screen. Christmas lights sparkled brightly outside her window, not to be outdone by the stars poking through the sky's dark blanket in wonder.

By the time the morning's shift began taking over, Kate was already into her third cup of coffee and making excellent progress. Her thoughts of the four days with Zach fueled her imagination. It seemed like a distant memory, something that had happened in another time. Sometimes, marveling at the seemingly perfect moments and conversation, she wondered if she hadn't indeed made it up. Mostly, though, Kate just let the overarching feelings of warmth, comfort, and hope wash over her. It was enough knowing he was out there somewhere. She peered out her window, catching a glimpse of Venus peeking up over the horizon. She wondered what planets he could see. Was he out there watching too?

She settled back into her seat and stretched

her back, rubbing her neck as she closed her eyes, still seeing stars. When she opened them again, her gaze fell to her notes written and spread out on the dinette table next to her laptop. She began moving them around and saw the battered edge of the worn and creased wine trail map. She reached for it, then ran her finger along the thin black winding line that represented Highway 290.

She smiled, thinking of all the stories and lives that tiny line represented. Then she thought of all the roads she had taken in the past. All the other thin winding lines that connect somehow across the vast tapestry of this country's terrain. She thought of Lillie. What line was she on right now?

Kate shook her head and decided her break had been long enough. Digging back in, she continued stringing words together and filling the endless blank pages until the sun shone full, reflecting off every surface of the trailer. The

green and red Christmas Cactus stood proudly
watching from the kitchen counter.

———

"So, TELL ME HOW it's going?" Caroline asked
into the phone.

Kate stepped outside of her trailer and marveled at the Texas weather. She could be freez-
ing in the morning and wearing a T-shirt and
flip-flops by afternoon. "Good," she said. "I may
actually get done before my deadline, if you can
believe that."

"Fantastic!" Caroline said and then turned
away from the receiver and Kate could hear a
commotion in the background of voices and
clanking noises.

"What's going on over there?" Kate asked as
she sat back into a bright red Adirondack chair
and shielded her eyes from the overhead glare.

"Oh, we are up to our eyeballs in dough,"
Caroline said, exasperated. "I don't know why
every year I think it's a good idea to make sugar

cookies. They are so time-consuming and such a mess." Although she complained, Kate knew her friend secretly loved it.

"Yes, but when else would you get to use that fabulous retro mixer?"

"Oh, Lord, let's see if I can just remember the lovely soul who gave me that for a wedding gift years ago . . ."

"Oh, just a very wise woman." They both laughed.

"So, speaking of wise," Caroline prodded, "have you wised up and decided to call Dr. Wine yet?"

Kate smiled into the phone, shaking her head. Caroline was like a dog with a bone. "No. But I have woven him into my story line and I am absolutely in love with him. I mean it." Kate grinned as she corrected her statement. "If I can't live it in real life, I may as well live vicariously through my own characters!"

She heard Caroline laugh on the other end.

"Well, I can't wait to read it, darlin'. By the way, have you thought about what you are going to do once the draft is done? Isn't your rental up in January?"

"Well, I was thinking about heading your way and maybe crashing at the beach for a bit?"

Caroline squealed through the phone, "YAS! Oh, my Lawd, we would *love* to have you! The guesthouse is all ready for you anytime."

"Well, I'm not sure for how long. It sort of depends on the novel publishing and then the tour . . ."

Caroline didn't pry and just restated, "Girl, you are welcome anytime and for however long. You are family. Besides, I could use some girl time. Bring me some of that fancy Texas wine when you come and we can have ourselves a hootenanny!"

"You got it!" Kate said with a laugh.

"Tell me," Caroline started, her tone shifting, "what are you doing for Christmas this year?"

Kate took a deep breath. "I actually think I'm going to do something different. Just like this whole trip has been totally different, trading snow for cactus heat. I've decided to spend the holiday on the gulf. Headed to Mustang Island and Port Aransas."

"Ooh! That sounds lovely!"

"Yes, I figured celebrating Christmas Day with the ocean waves, sun, and sand will be a nice change from the rainy Northwest," Kate said, proud of her new plan.

Caroline agreed, "That's a wonderful idea. And I can't wait to see you on our side of the gulf soon."

They hung up and Kate smiled at the thought of how much Caroline was like family. She had been there through all the ups and downs over the past twenty years, and they were still thick as thieves. She laughed, thinking about how it all started from a work friendship. Who knew back then that they were paving the way to a shared future? Those deep roots started with just a little seed of friendship. Kate felt gratitude deep in her heart for her soul sister. She wasn't sure she could have weathered the storms of her life without her. It certainly wouldn't have been as much fun. She got up and headed back to the trailer to finish her work for the day and prepare for the journey to the beach.

⇉ Fourteen ⇇

CHRISTMAS DAY

K ate sat in a rainbow beach chair looking out onto the seafoam waves gently rolling to shore. She had driven down from the Hill Country to the gulf yesterday. On a whim, she chose to camp on the beach at Port Aransas rather than check into a hotel.

Not much of a camper at all, Kate instead slept in her car, as did many other revelers celebrating this time of year. Waking up early this morning, she watched the sun rise bright orange and beautiful, slowly ascending majestically above the horizon. It was peaceful and calm, and she watched the shore birds waiting patiently for whatever breakfast treats arrived on the incoming waves. Truly, this was a different kind of Christmas than she had ever spent, and she breathed in the salt air, letting it soothe her soul.

Taking a break from the relentless pace of her writing, Kate felt a bit untethered without her routine. Yet she told herself to pay attention to this moment now, as it would likely be a while before she found herself on these shores again.

She saw the freighters and drilling rigs poking up in the water in the far distance, and then brought her gaze closer. She would play a game, catching one part of a wave and then following it with her eyes as it rolled and moved along, picking up speed until it crashed onto the wet sand into a foaming fury before getting pulled backward with the tide.

Kate had always felt an affinity for water. Any water would do, but particularly oceans. There was something so mercurial about the tug and pull, and the endless roaring waves and sand made their way into every crevice of her being, settling her down. It was always like coming home.

Home. Where would she live after this adventure? She looked forward to spending time with Caroline in Pensacola, and to soak in quality time with her dear friend. What then?

Her thoughts were like the waves, flitting back and forth, never staying in one place for too long. She thought about David, and she imagined him celebrating with his family in Charleston. A year ago she would never have dreamed that she would be spending another Christmas holiday alone. David's large family would fill in the gaps with their cacophony. She had clung to those family get-togethers. Family by marriage. She had hoped that he would rescue her from the loneliness of her own family's shortcomings.

Her mother. Every year at this time, she was brought right back to that darkened hospice room and the sharp, antiseptic smell. In her final moments, she was heavily sedated with morphine, and Kate wasn't sure she knew she was there. Her mother's frame was dwarfed by the bed as she was curled up in a ball, as though praying for release. Lillie was sitting silently on the other side of the bed.

It wasn't like those movies of families who come together at the end and the mother tells them some poignant thing before drifting off to the ever after, the bonds of the family restored. Instead, it was an awkward moment filled with red-rimmed eyes and the whooshing sounds of the ventilator expanding and contracting. In the end, Kate followed her mother's wishes, and then she and Lillie drifted apart again, Kate returning to Charleston, Lillie to France.

Back on the beach, Kate was left alone with her thoughts. They scurried around like the sandpipers, nervously hunting in the sand for their next morsel.

She felt that pain of longing in her heart and wondered if she would ever feel whole again. She knew that her decision to leave David was the right one, but it didn't erase the pain of losing. Kate felt that double-edged sword keenly as she examined and reexamined her choices.

Why is it that the one who leaves is to blame? she wondered. In fact, Kate felt that leaving had been a much harder decision than just pretending that nothing was wrong and turning a blind eye. But she was still young. Too young, in fact, to give up on her dreams. What about her life in the future?

She thought about the older couple from

the winery and how they relished their years together. What a wonderful gift that would be. To have "found" the love of your life so young, and to have such a long time together. Then she thought of other couples she knew who were also together a long time, but living separate lives. The marriages were just a convenient way to fit in with the rest of society. These couples hid their true feelings behind masks of booze and pills. To everyone else they appeared to be in love, because that's what married couples are supposed to be, right? But behind closed doors, they disappeared to separate chambers in the same house. Living out their years in bitter acceptance.

This wasn't the kind of marriage Kate had wanted. She had been lured into David's fantastic world, which was exciting and heady. But the reality was she would be just as happy finding someone to sit next to her right now on the beach and enjoy the beautiful sunrise in complete silence.

Truthfully, she had been tripped up by her own ego. She thought she could marry away her past losses and be elevated to David's status in one swoop. She wanted that fame. She wanted to finally be recognized for her work and to show the world, "See, I am someone important because he chose me!"

She was embarrassed by her own need to feed her ego.

How silly it all seemed now. As if she could just step into someone else's life and leave her own with a name change.

Yet, isn't that how it works? She was raised expecting to marry someone someday and assume his name. That her life wouldn't be complete without this.

What happens when it doesn't work the way everyone says it should? What happens when you don't meet the love of your life and you instead end up in midlife alone?

How do you live after leaving?

It was useless to run scenarios over and over through her mind. Yet, Kate continued, it was never far from her thoughts. She wrestled with the guilt, pain, and shame of her decision daily.

The hardest part is believing the lie that if she had stayed, they could have worked it out. For some people, this may be true. For her and David, it was not. They had an agreement from the start, that if he played games and wasn't honest with her, she would leave him. For them it was a love later in life, and with it came much baggage.

Kate finally had to accept that she couldn't change anyone's opinion of her decision. That this was a choice she had to make for herself and stand by it. She stood, looking out into the great expanse of the sea stretching in front of her, and felt her solitude buffeted by each gust of salty wind.

Her thoughts shifted to and settled on Zach. She breathed deeply, letting out a heavy sigh as she remembered his tender touch. She didn't know whether she could believe or hope again for love. She wanted to be optimistic, but instead felt the weight of her life so far.

Still, she turned their short time together over and over in her mind. She walked a distance toward the wet sand and picked up a delicate shell. She followed the blue and white ridges with her fingertips, marveling at how this shell made it through all the turbulence, the rocky bottom, the changing tides, and arrived completely intact at her feet. Perhaps love was like that as well? That we launch ourselves over and over into the seas of life, to be battered by the waves and weather. Some of us remain intact, while others are broken.

Yet we keep returning. To do it again and again.

Kate laughed to herself at the absurdity of it all. She didn't have any answers, only observations.

As she watched seven pelicans glide slowly just inches above the waterline, cruising gracefully in a row, she smiled. Sometimes it does work. Sometimes we do find our way home. It just may not look the way we expect.

She smiled at this thought and listened to kids screaming playfully off in the distance, while a small white-and-black terrier ran into the waves chasing after a gull. A couple of golf carts cruised by full of people shouting "Merry Christmas!" or "*¡Feliz Navidad!*" Kate waved at them and thought that there was no other place she'd rather be in the world than right here, right now.

Kate turned back to her SUV, opening the passenger door to reach inside for her cell phone. She untethered it from the charging cord and saw that she had some missed call notifications, likely from Caroline. There was someone else she needed to talk to right now more than anything. She scrolled through her text messages until she found the name and hit the phone icon to place the call.

A few moments later, she heard the ringing. Three rings later, a voice answered, "Hello?"

"Lillie. Merry Christmas!" Kate said. Lillie cleared her throat and responded, "Merry Christmas to you too, Kate."

Kate could hear her rustling around as she asked, "Where are you now?"

"We're in Biarritz, just off the Basque coast of France."

"Oh, I bet that is beautiful. How is your tour?" Kate asked.

Lillie's voice was muffled for a moment, then clearly, "Oh, it's going well. We are eating dinner now and then have a gig later this evening."

Kate hesitated. "Well, I don't want to keep you, but I just wanted to wish you a Merry Christmas."

"Are you in Charleston?" Lillie asked before taking another bite.

"Um, no. I'm on the beach in Port Aransas, Texas." She trailed off, unsure how to explain to her younger sister about the separation.

"Oh, neat! I bet that's a lot warmer than here," Lillie replied.

Kate let silence fill the line for a moment. "I know this is a difficult time for us, but I really miss you. Will you be coming back Stateside next year?"

A kite was being flown up the beach, and Kate watched the red tail duck and swirl in the wind gusts, tempting the ground.

"Yeah, me too. It just depends on our tour schedule," Lillie replied.

Kate just nodded into the phone but felt discouraged. Since their mother had passed, their bond had slowly deteriorated over the years. Part of this was due to the fact of her own busy tour schedule, then marriage. They were like passing ships, never in the same location at the same time.

Now more than ever, Kate wanted to bridge that gap.

"Well, I wish you the merriest of Christmas-es, and hope that this coming new year is full of everything you desire," Kate said.

"You too, sis," Lillie said.

Kate reluctantly pressed the red button to end the call and was brought back to the beach.

The sounds of seabirds calling sharply back and forth. Kids' delightful laughter piercing through the crashing wall of waves. A golf cart whizzing by with a boom box playing Christmas tunes, "Have a holly, jolly Christmas . . ." Kate let her longing settle deep into her chest, and she wiped the tears from her cheeks.

She really did hope to see Lillie, and she

knew this year would be different. Kate realized that the fear she felt not knowing where she would go next was really freedom in disguise. Her options were as unlimited as the vast ocean. Rather than feel the loss, she needed to see the flip side of the coin. There were endless possibilities. Perhaps this was the beginning rather than the end?

Kate stood taller, stretching her arms into that endless space. The sunlight sparkled off the water, beautiful and beckoning her closer. She walked to the edge of the waterline and let the remnants of waves gently caress her feet, the cold water startling and refreshing. She walked along for a bit, taking in all of nature's beauty, stopping every now and then to dig for treasure. She saw the edge of an oyster shell and gently dug into the sand to free it. One half empty without a pearl, it was still beautiful. The layers encrusted with sand. Shades of purple, gray, and white swirled to the center. Kate rinsed it in the tide, then took it with her. She may be half a shell now, but she knew that was okay. She was enough.

Just like this shell, she was well worn with time and tide. Still beautiful, inside and out.

In time she would find her other half. For now she would have this shell as a reminder of this beautiful Christmas on the gulf.

⇒ Fifteen ⇐

NEW YEAR'S EVE

Kate couldn't believe it. She had finished her draft, and she actually liked it. For the first time in a long while, she felt her writing just pour out naturally. It felt like an extension of herself, and she was extremely proud to share her story with the world. Her words. Her voice. Her truths.

Kate smiled warmly, feeling like something

had permanently shifted in her during these past three months. The Texas sun, heat, and dust just settled into her bones in a way she would never be able to forget. She had started off this trip hurting, a little lost, and feeling a lot of guilt over her life choices and her book deadline. She laughed to herself as she rolled up a sweater to stuff inside her duffel bag. Now she felt free. There was something in the act of letting go. Letting go of the voices of doubt, discouragement, and condemnation. About focusing solely on her art. Believing in herself that she could tap back into what she loved. Before the marriage. Before she was an "us." It was as though the gusty winds that blew against her trailer shook loose her dry bones, revealing new life. She finally felt as though she deserved to move forward. That she had a future. That she was in control of herself in a way that she would never relinquish to anyone else again.

Most importantly, she forgave herself. She

understood that she could only take responsibility for her own actions. That meant she had
to love herself all that much more. She couldn't
wait around for someone else to rescue her or
do it for her. She had everything within herself.
She had the power.

She grabbed at her pile of clothing and saw
the pink V-neck sweater she had worn that last
day with Zach. She pulled it close to her, breath-
ing into it, wondering if she could still catch a
hint of his scent. Laughing to herself, she closed
her eyes and held the sweater up to her cheek,
remembering how lovely it felt to glide about
in his arms, to feel his breath against hers. She
shuddered with remembrance and opened her
eyes back up to continue folding and rolling the
sweater, placing it into the waiting bag.

Zach was certainly a huge part of this shift.
The way Kate thought about it, there are people
who come into your life for a reason. We don't
always know what that reason is. Sometimes

it's to stay. Sometimes it's to learn a lesson. Sometimes it's to remind us of something we have forgotten long ago. Some buried treasure within our hearts that we can't get to unless we have help.

Zach was that help. He reminded Kate that anything is possible. That hope is not wasted. That love is real.

More than anything, he showed her that she was worth loving. She was enough, right now. That she had a purpose and a calling to write, and that she could do it on her own.

Trust. This season taught her to trust herself. Trust that she was making the right decisions for her future, that even though the decisions may not make sense to others, that ultimately she could trust her own heart and soul for guidance.

She continued packing things for her departure to Pensacola, and then took a break close to midnight. She had stowed most of the other bottles of wine to share with Caroline once she got there. One bottle she had saved to celebrate the New Year: 2017 Adoration, a pinot noir rosé from Heath Sparkling Wines. Adoration stands for deep love and respect. That is how Kate felt about her time here in Texas. As she popped the cork and poured the rose, gold-hued liquid into a wineglass, she felt overwhelming gratitude in this precise moment.

She wondered what David was doing. As if on cue, a text message lit up her iPhone screen with a buzz notification.

"You could be celebrating here with me. Have you figured out yet that we are meant to be together? Come home. It's not too late."

Kate laughed at the absurdity of his moods: one moment hating her, and the next professing true love. She felt in herself a new confidence. Maybe it was the satisfaction from finishing her next book. Or the fact that she felt she could go on without him. That it wasn't about him, but about her discovering her true path.

Either way, she felt pleased that she no longer questioned her choice. And she wasn't about to let his texts burst her bubble any longer.

"That's your story. I'm still writing mine. I've signed the papers your lawyer sent and emailed them back. Happy New Year, David."

She clicked her phone dark and held the glass up in the air as the clock on the microwave lit up 12:00. She could hear fireworks in the distance, and cheers from within some of the other trailers nearby. Kate laughed and toasted to the New Year. A year full of possibility, joy, happiness, and magic. As she sipped the berry-infused bubbles, she said a quiet prayer for Zach. That he was happy, healthy, and loved.

⇒ Sixteen ⇐

NINE MONTHS LATER

"It was then that she knew, she had always known, that he was her guiding star. That even though he may be far away in the midnight sky, he would always shine brightly for her. Illuminating her path. Reminding her that dreams do come true."

Kate finished reading to applause and looked out over the rows of seats filled with smiling faces at the Union Square Barnes & Noble. She had dreamed of this moment. Coming back to the top floor of this bookstore in the heart of New York City where she had been overwhelmingly welcomed during her first book tour. It was fall in the city, and Kate was cozy in a red oversized turtleneck sweater that contrasted nicely with the black frames of her glasses and her brilliant blond hair under the bright glare of the spotlights. She thanked everyone and then began answering moderated questions.

A woman stood in the audience as one of the helpers handed her a microphone. "Hi, Kate. We know most fiction is based on fact, and I was wondering how much of this is based on your real life."

Kate smiled from her seat. "Thank you. Well, yes. Most of my novel is based on real experiences I've had, but it's not autobiographical. I tend to weave the bits and pieces of my life together to make it much more exciting than my real life." Kate laughed. "But the stories I write highlight the lessons I've learned and hope to share with others."

The woman sat down and another younger woman raised her hand and the helper hurried to hand her the microphone. "Kate, can you tell us if there really was a Dr. Wine?"

Kate smiled warmly. "Well, that wasn't his name, of course. But yes, that experience was real, and although I embellished quite a bit in the novel, his effect on me was very real and lasting."

The woman smiled in excitement as she sat down and another question was asked, this time by a man. "Hi, Kate. I just want you to know how much I appreciate your writing. I'm also a wine lover, so I look forward to making my way to the wine trail next year. Do you know what you will write next? Will there be a sequel?"

"I'm not exactly sure yet whether there will be a sequel to this novel." She looked over to her agent for approval before continuing. "But we are in negotiations with our publisher and hoping to announce by the end of the year."

The moderator thanked everyone for coming and thanked Kate for her reading. They finished to applause and Kate stood, shaking the moderator's hand, and then made her way to the table with stacks of her books to be signed for the readers lining up in the aisle.

It was an hour later when she and her agent, Margaret, stepped through the heavy ornate brass doors of the bookstore to meet the brisk city air outside. Union Square was alive with activity. Shoppers bustling about, coming up and down the subway steps, and streaming out onto Fourteenth Street. Fall in New York City. It was the perfect time of year as the trees began to shed their leaves, the crispness of the air only adding to the excitement and anticipation of the coming holiday season. Everyone was in good spirits, and Kate shivered in the thrill of it all, pulling her cashmere coat and scarf closer around her neck.

"Shall we grab a drink?" Margaret asked her, to which Kate nodded emphatically.

"I'm parched! How about the Grey Dog?"

They stepped out onto the sidewalk and into the steady flow of pedestrians. Kate gingerly sidestepped cracks in the paving stones as she took in the whole scene. She had forgotten how infectious the energy of the city was. Even though she hadn't slept much, as this tour had been particularly grueling, she felt completely wide awake once outside. They made their way the two long blocks to the small café, where they ducked inside and grabbed a small round table on the other side of a velvet curtain designed to keep the chilly air out. The café had been one of Kate's favorite haunts as a student at NYU, and she thrived on the creative energy that emanated from all the students and city dwellers who made it a regular stop.

"Cabernet, right?" Margaret asked as she stepped up to the counter to order, returning a short time later with two full glasses of red wine.

"Cheers! Let's toast to a magnificent tour!" Margaret said emphatically and they clinked glasses across the table.

Kate took a sip, then settled back into her seat, loosening her scarf. "Wow. What a trip it's been. It is so good to be back here."

Margaret nodded. "Yes, we have really missed you." She took a sip and then continued, "You know, last year I wasn't sure if you were going to make your deadline."

Kate laughed. "Me neither! I was really sweating it, and not at all inspired to write about anything," she added honestly. "I mean, I really didn't think anyone would want to read anything I had to say."

"Yes, but you believed in yourself and pulled through. And you have proven once again that you are an author worthy of all this." She gestured as if taking in the whole city.

"I know it was risky changing genres, but I have to say that I've never felt more comfortable in my own skin as a writer," Kate said, beaming.

"Well, secretly, I knew that you could pull it off. You just needed to have confidence in yourself." Margaret winked.

"Well, I finally got some help in the inspiration department. That trip to Texas really changed so much of my mind-set. And I am so grateful to you for your guidance and patience." Kate smiled at her friend.

"It was, and is, my pleasure, Kate." Margaret lifted her glass to take another sip, then gestured to her. "So what are you going to do now that your tour has ended? Vacation? Beach time? I'd love to get a break from this cold and head to Punta Cana or somewhere else nice and warm."

Kate smiled to herself as she knew exactly

where she wanted to be. "I think I'll take some of this royalty money burning a hole in my bank account and make an investment."

Margaret raised her eyebrows. "On what?"

"A home. Well, an Airstream, to be exact."

Margaret looked at her as only a city dweller would do. "You aren't thinking of living in one, are you?"

"Why not? Most of the trailers I've seen have more room than an SRO on the Upper West Side!"

They both laughed in agreement. "True, but what about where you park it?"

"Well, if we do get this deal sorted out for a sequel, I will need to head back to the wine trail. I figured I'd find another park outside of Austin where I could sort of pick back up where I left off."

Margaret regarded her with a sideways smirk. "And perhaps run into your Dr. Wine in the process?"

"Oh, I don't think that will happen. I mean, it was insanely magical, but how many shooting stars will one get to see in a lifetime?" Kate asked.

Margaret just shrugged and smiled, because even though she was somewhat jaded by the big city, she was still a romantic at heart. Most New Yorkers are. Kate thought about her odds, and then brushed it off. Maybe she was heading back to the scene of the crime, so to speak, but she had to believe that Zach was still in the Northeast.

Kate remembered fondly how being in Texas made her feel like home. She felt as though she finally belonged. And the idea of getting to be that much closer again to all those warm memories was another attractive reason to go. "When will you know about the contract?" Kate asked Margaret.

"We should know by Monday morning. I am confident that you can make your plans accordingly. This novel far exceeded their estimations, and I know that everyone is looking forward to hearing what happens next. Myself included!"

Kate laughed. "Well, that makes two of us. I can't wait to see what sort of magic I can drum up. This last year far surpassed my own expectations. I have a good feeling about the sequel."

Kate looked out the window to watch the hurry of bundled-up shoppers whisking past. She turned to Margaret and finished her last sip of wine. "Well, I'm headed back to the hotel, and then flying to Pensacola in the morning."

They stood and bundled up for a moment before Margaret pulled Kate close for a hug. "Kate, I really am so grateful you chose me as your agent. I couldn't be more proud to have you as one of my writers. And I know this is just the beginning for you."

Kate blushed under the warmth. "Margaret, you have been a godsend. Thank you again for all your support and love over the years." They embraced once more before heading out the door and in opposite directions.

⇒ Seventeen ⇐

Kate stirred in the morning light, reluctantly letting go of the deep clutches from a
vivid dream. She willed her eyes open and for
a moment was completely disoriented. Used to
the blackout curtains of hotels, the bright light
streaming through the transparent white curtains revealed her place in time. It all flooded
back in an instant. Caroline's.

   She smiled and stretched underneath the
covers, taking a moment to fully wake before
trying to sit up. She had absolutely no idea what

time it was. The wonderful thing about a brick guesthouse was that she heard no sounds from the main house. For all she knew, she could be marooned on an island with the quiet that surrounded her.

A mockingbird called out and she roused herself, knowing that today was the day she would pick up her new trailer. She grabbed her phone from the bedside table and flipped it over: 8:16 a.m. *Not too bad*, she thought. She felt like she had slept much longer.

She sat up in bed fumbling for her flip-flops and then stood stretching in the sunlight. She grabbed a robe from behind the bathroom door, then headed toward the exit as if her life depended on it: coffee.

She gently opened the door to the main house and immediately smelled the French roast mixed with . . . was that beignets? *Oh my gosh*, Kate thought. *Why would I ever leave this place?*

Straightening her robe, she shuffled down

the long hallway, then turned the curve into the kitchen, honing in on the coffeemaker like a homing pigeon.

"Well, good morning, sunshine!" Caroline greeted her from the island. She was sifting through the morning paper, sipping black coffee from her mother's rose-patterned china cup.

"I slept like the dead," Kate declared as she poured herself a cup and then fetched some cream from the fridge. "I never sleep that well on hotel beds, so this was a long time coming."

Caroline smirked. "Well, you'd better enjoy it because soon you'll be cramped in your little metal capsule, missing our heavenly down bedding!"

Her eyes crinkled above her bright red readers. Kate shook her head. "I know. I know." She took a long sip of coffee, then added, "What kind of normal person decides to willingly move into a hundred-and-fifty-square-foot aluminum egg?" She grabbed a powdered sugar-covered beignet off the plate and shoved the delicious donut into her mouth.

"Why don't we take our coffee on the back porch?" Caroline suggested as she got up and Kate nodded, following. Heck, she'd follow her anywhere as long as she could drink more of this nectar.

She loved this porch. It was decorated with original wicker chairs and a couch. Tucked between the weavings of white poked out the greenest ferns bedded inside gorgeous blue and white ceramic pots. Every spot beckoned you to stay longer. Completely screened in, it gave you the sense of privacy without sacrificing air flow. And, of course, it kept the pesky mosquitoes from ruining a perfectly good time.

Caroline took a moment to get situated, then enjoyed a long gulp before meeting Kate's eyes.

"So tell me. How are you?" she asked pointedly.

Kate laughed defensively at first, then

remembered that this was her dear friend whom she had nothing to hide from.

"Actually, I'm really good. I can't remember feeling this happy or healthy."

Caroline nodded in agreement. "Yes, I was thinking the same thing last night. You have this glow about you that I haven't seen in a very long time." She smiled warmly. "I just wanted to be sure we had time to really connect before you head out again."

Kate so appreciated her friend. "Yes. I'm really going to miss our time together. I've really felt like part of your family." Kate thought about the festivities from the previous night. Caroline, Rob, and their beautiful children Remi and Leah. They had popped popcorn and laughed together, catching up around the blazing light from their outdoor firepit until the wee hours of the night.

"You are Auntie Kate!" Caroline insisted.

Kate laughed and truly felt the sentiment.

"Yes, I know you say that, but honestly I've felt like a stranger in a strange land for far too long. It just felt really and truly good to finally belong."

Caroline reached over to squeeze the back of Kate's hand. "And you always will."

Kate felt the rush of love and warmth overwhelm her, and she looked away for a moment as hot tears threatened in the corners of her eyes. She breathed deeply and focused her attention on the large green elephant ear plants intently listening on the other side of the screen.

She tuned back to Caroline's voice. "I know that you had a really rough go of this, but I'm wondering how you feel now?"

Kate took a deep breath and focused her thoughts. "Honestly, for a long time I was really obsessed with what everyone thought of me. Maybe I was too focused on this. I gave everyone power over my own story. What I finally realized is that the spell can be broken. I mean, you think that these people and your feelings have all this control over you, and that this is true love, and that you will never ever be free from the pain of the loss. But then you realize that you've had the power all along. That no one can take that away from you unless you give it to them."

"Absolutely," Caroline said. "No one really knows the whole story but you and David. Folks are always quick to judge what they fear the most. It's really just a reflection of their own insecurities. Who gives a hoot what anyone thinks about you? I mean, we pride ourselves on being loving and open in the South, but honestly, I've never met more backstabbing people in my life. And these are some of my dearest friends!" They both laughed.

"Listen, in the end, all that matters is that you are living a life you can be proud of. A life that is true to yourself. I'm so darn proud of you, Kate. That you stood up for yourself, even when it meant standing alone sometimes," Caroline said before draining her cup.

Kate smiled and nodded before finishing hers. "Thank you. I mean, it makes perfect sense to hear, but I think it's much harder for us to practice. We all want to be loved and to fit in. For some people it's easier than others."

Kate pondered this for a moment before adding, "You know, meeting Zach was a pivotal moment for me. Having someone believe in me like that without wanting anything in return. That was a powerful push for me to believe in myself."

"It's high time you did. I've always felt that you were your own shining star," Caroline said before adding, "I have a hard time believing that's the end of that story. You had to have met for a reason."

"Well, I guess we'll find out. But for now I am beyond thrilled to take the proceeds from my novel and start a new life in my Airstream in the Hill Country," Kate said.

Kate peered into her empty coffee cup. "It's probably time for me to get ready and pack up."

"Oh, Lawd. I mean, I just wish you'd get out of my hair already," Caroline said, laughing sarcastically. "I'd have more coffee to drink."

They moved closer and embraced one another firmly and for a long time. Kate could smell the lavender soap on Caroline's skin. She held onto her like a lifeline until they finally broke apart.

"Now, listen. You have a whole life of adventures ahead of you." She held her hand to Kate's cheek. "And don't you dare let anyone hold you back. Remember, when the right fit comes along, you'll just know. It will all be so easy and effortless. Like coming home. But there's no rush." Caroline squeezed her friend closer before pulling away again.

"To adventures!" Kate exclaimed, raising her empty cup toward the ceiling fans above, lazily pushing against the humid heat.

They laughed and walked together back to the main house, arm in arm.

The only thing that could separate Kate from her dear friend was the reality that her new shiny home on wheels was a few hours away. It was time for her to start this next chapter of her life.

⇒ Eighteen ⇐

Kate sat inside her Durango in the parking lot of the Airstream dealership in Gulfport, Mississippi. Her engine hummed, and as she adjusted the rearview mirror, it reflected the large metal tube shining behind her.

It had taken most of the day to get the walk-through tour of the trailer, hitch installed, and the final paperwork completed. Kate was exhausted from the tour and the drive from Pensacola, but her adrenaline fueled her on. She was beyond pleased at how the trailer looked.

Clean lines with beautiful accents. She couldn't wait to stow her items in all the compartments. What adventures she had ahead of her!

She hummed the Kacey Musgraves tune "Who needs a house up on a hill when you can have one on four wheels . . ."

She pulled forward slowly at first, feeling the tug of her new home solidly attached. It felt comfortable. She turned out of the driveway onto Highway 49, then slowly picked up speed. "Here we go!" Kate exclaimed. She could see the reflection of her rig as she passed the dealership's windows and smiled as it looked picture perfect.

About fifty miles later, she pulled into the RV park just as the sun was starting to set. She was nervous about setting up in the dark, so the owner of the park kindly guided her to her spot near the office. Her first time backing in, she rolled down her window and leaned out while he stood behind and gently helped her

ease the trailer back into alignment with the
driver's side hookups.

Thankfully, he had a flashlight with him, and
helped talk her through the process of lowering
the electric hitch and leveling the trailer. He
was very patient with Kate, not trying to take
over, knowing that she would have to do this
herself in the future and needed to practice on
her own. She then pulled out all the accessories
and hurriedly opened up the boxes and untethered the hoses. He gave her some tips, such as
hooking up her water hose to the post first and
getting the air out before attaching it to her
trailer. And not to flip the electric breaker on
until her cable was securely hooked up to the
surge protector and her trailer.

By the time they finished, it was dark. Kate
thanked him profusely, then settled herself
inside the cabin, turning on the interior lights.
She sat at the dinette for a moment, just taking
it all in. Her bags of bedding were thrown on

top of the bed. Kitchen gear still in the car. She was exhausted, but elated.

"Hello, little home!" She smiled warmly and ran her fingertips along the shiny edges of the tabletop. It smelled like a new trailer—sharp, fresh, and wonderful. The leather seats gave a little, and she knew they would soon be worn into a comfortable degree.

Taking a deep breath, she realized that she had done it. She had bought a trailer, towed it, backed it up, and unhitched it.

There were going to be so many more "firsts," but this one was especially sweet, and she savored the moment. The only thing she still had left to do was grab the bottle of wine from her car and toast to her new future.

She laughed to herself and made this the first priority, over putting things away. Looking at the black, red, and white label of the Ron Yates Tempranillo, Kate felt warm with the thought that she was headed back.

She uncorked it, then poured herself a healthy serving in her new plastic camper-safe stemless wineglass.

"Here's to our many adventures ahead!" Then she looked upward and said out loud, "Thank you! I know you are watching over me, and I couldn't have done this without you." She smiled, held her glass up in the air, then took a healthy sip, letting the rich red warm her on the inside.

Kate knew that she had so much to learn. So many things yet to do. Yet she also knew that she had time. That she just needed to take it step by step, moment by moment. That it would all come together.

Most of all, she knew that she could do this. That satisfaction washed over her with a profound sense of respect that comes from doing the hard things and proving to yourself that you can.

"Texas, here we come!" She laughed, and

took another sip in the warm and cozy cabin
of her new home.

⇉ Nineteen ⇇

Kate had decided to spend a few days in Mississippi just to be sure she didn't have any major issues before heading out on the long trip to Texas. She tried out every appliance, and made multiple trips to the local stores to fetch items she needed. She was surprised by how comfortable the mattress was, and actually enjoyed reading from the cozy nook at night.

She utilized the park's Wi-Fi, rewatching her saved videos and then tackling the chores in real life. Handling the combined gray-and-black tank and attaching it to the park's sewer system wasn't as bad as she initially thought, but she was glad to have her vinyl blue gloves on. She settled into every space, and then pulled out her atlas to chart her trip back to the Hill Country. She would, of course, rely on her GPS, but she still loved to see the whole plan unfold before her on paper. There was something really visceral about seeing the topography, tracing her finger along the tiny lines as she found her desired path back.

She chatted with Caroline a few times and sent some pictures of the trailer once she had it all set up. Of course, her friend was thrilled. It seemed like a week had passed since they had been together on that porch, when it had only been two days. *I suppose that's what happens when you are trying new things*, Kate thought. It was stressful in an entirely different way.

Her last mission was to hitch the trailer by herself, and that still terrified her to some degree. On her last morning, she took the final sip from her coffee mug and drained the rest in the sink. She was resolved to do it.

Standing outside at the tongue of the trailer, she pressed the button to make the hitch get taller. When she was finally satisfied that it was higher than the ball on her bumper, she got into her Durango, took a deep breath, and backed it up slowly, using the rear camera as guidance.

It was painstaking. An hour later and a million inches back and forth, Kate was completely frustrated and ready to just drive off and leave the trailer there. That, or move permanently into this campsite for good.

She felt hot tears pressing against her eyes as she blinked them away. "I can do this. People do this all the time. Women do this all the time." She brushed off the instinct to run into the office to ask for help, and instead took a moment in the car to collect herself.

She had time. She just had to overcome her

fear of doing it wrong, and instead see it happening. She closed her eyes and visualized the ball lining up slowly right underneath the socket. She opened her eyes and took a deep breath.

Kate, you can do this.

She put the Durango into drive to pull forward and line herself up more squarely, then she put it into reverse and slowly began to creep back toward the trailer. This time she just breathed through it and watched the ball in the camera, willing it to go right into the intended spot. When she saw the shadow creep over, she put it into park and hopped outside.

Bingo! It was perfectly lined up. She lowered the electric jack down and then clicked it into place, threading the safety pin through the holes and securing it.

Yes! She pumped her arms in the air in victory before attaching the swing arms and chains. She was spent by the time she had stowed all the gear and was ready to pull out onto the highway. *Towing isn't for the faint of heart*, she thought.

She'd do better next time. But at least she did it.

Setting the destination in her GPS, she did one more walk-around of the car and trailer before getting back into the driver's seat to pull out.

She thought of all the wonderful wine that was waiting for her. The beautiful dry scenery, the warm sun. She smiled to herself and said, "Giddy up!" Sliding the gear to drive, she pulled her little house forward and watched the miles tick down as she made her way across the South toward Texas.

⇉ Twenty ⇇

Kate had fully embraced her Airstream lifestyle. She went back to Open Air Resorts to
rent a monthly spot next to the other "full-tim-
ers." It was the holiday season again and she had
been working on her sequel in the cozy confines
of her dinette. Taking a break, she looked up
through the tinted windows and could see a
couple with two kids moving into her old rental
trailer across the park. It was like coming full
circle, yet she was in a completely different

place than a year ago. She had grown into the confident writer she had always aspired to be.

She checked the clock: noon.

Perfect time to head to Fredericksburg for some holiday shopping and wine tasting, she thought.

Driving back down the winding roads, Kate marveled at how quickly she had grown accustomed to her new life. Of course, the space was an adjustment. But she found a sense of security knowing that she had everything she needed and could hitch up and go at a moment's notice.

As she navigated back down 290 she felt that familiar tug of memories from the year before. What a wonderful time she had exploring the wineries with Zach. What a different place she had been in at that time. A time full of difficult decisions, questioning herself, and striking out on her own. She remembered how scared and unsure she had been. How she had been so blocked in writing, and unconvinced she could write a fiction novel, or any book again.

Yet here she was in the aftermath of a wonderful book tour, and her novel was listed on the *New York Times* best-seller list. She was excited to work on the sequel, and it seemed apropos that she came back to the Hill Country to do that.

Her heart? She felt that the turmoil of the separation and divorce was still relatively recent, but far enough in her rearview that she could see forward to a brighter future. It had been tough to disappoint so many people she loved. Yet she knew that this was an important step in growing up. If you are constantly living up to everyone else's expectations, you are merely a shadow of your true self.

This past year, Kate felt that she had finally stepped into her own light. She was writing again, and living a lifestyle she loved. Trailer life had taught her so many important lessons about simple living, resource management, and the importance of community. She loved getting to visit different parks and places, and she looked forward to doing a "trailer tour" when her sequel was released.

All in all, Kate felt at peace. She may be technically single, but she didn't feel alone. She was full of possibilities and instead focused on the rich lives of her characters as they came into existence with each word she wrote.

Kate passed the wooden fence of Pontotoc Vineyard. She found a parking spot and made her way into the shaded courtyard. The "Weingarten" sign still hung as she remembered from before, and she ordered a glass of Sangria and then settled in to appreciate the view.

Christmastime in Fredericksburg. This would be her new tradition, and she breathed in the beauty, magic, and wonder of it all. As she sipped the cold wine, she warmed herself with memories of talking to Zach about her childhood dreams. Laughing to herself, Kate spied a tall *Nutcracker* figure in the window and felt the tingle of anticipation and joy that this season promised. This year she felt even more hopeful.

Just then, her phone rang and she pulled it out to see it was Lillie.

"Hello!"

"Hi, *sis*!" Lillie replied. "I was hoping I could catch you before I went to sleep. How are things in Texas?"

"Sunny, warm, and festive," Kate replied. "I wish you were here to share this Sangria with me."

"Well, that's sort of why I'm calling . . ." Lillie paused. "I have decided to come back home—back to the States—after this tour is over."

Kate could hardly contain her excitement as she let her sister continue.

"I think I could use some time off, and also a warmer climate." She chuckled. "Besides, I LOVE your new book, and was thinking maybe it's time I check out the Wine Trail for myself?"

"Oh, my gosh, yes!! When could you come?" Kate said, beaming.

"Well, I actually was going to take a flight to Austin on New Year's Day. Would that be okay?" she asked.

"Oh, absolutely!" Kate exclaimed. "I can see if one of the Airstreams or cabin rentals is available for you. That would be amazing!"

"Great." Lillie sounded relieved. "It may only be for a week, but I'll send you the details of my flight and I can reimburse you for the rental."

"I would love to see you for however long you can stay," Kate enthused.

"That would be so amazing if I could stay in the same trailer you wrote your novel in!" Lillie added.

"I'll see what I can do. Oh, sis, I can't wait to see you!" Kate said.

"Me too. All right, I'll hang up now, but I'll text you and see you in a few weeks!" Lillie said.

"Sweet dreams, Lillie," Kate said before Lillie disconnected.

She stared at the blank phone in disbelief. Finally her sister was coming home. She had prayed for this for so long she thought that God wasn't listening anymore.

Thank you she breathed as she looked up to the blue skies peeking between the branches of a tall oak tree. Patience. She knew that she just had to trust and have patience that Lillie would eventually return.

Kate couldn't have thought of a more perfect Christmas gift.

She finished her Sangria, fueled now by the mission to find a rental for Lillie, and then begin preparations for her visit. Her head began to fill with food, wine, and presents. But first she wanted to see if she could purchase one of the beautiful handcarved *Nutcracker* figures for her trailer.

She ducked into a wooden building on one side of the courtyard and let her eyes adjust to the change in light. She found the rows of wooden figures against one wall and stepped over to examine each one, hoping to find the perfect mascot for her new Airstream home.

She had just picked up a smaller one with a red and white painted jacket and a tall golden crown when she heard behind her, "Um, excuse me, are you KB Summers?"

Kate turned around to see a lovely young woman with long, dark chestnut hair peering intently at her. "Yes, I am."

"Oh. My. God. I LOVE your novel!" the girl continued rapidly. "I loved every minute of it. Please tell me you are working on a sequel?"

Kate smiled as she thought of how proud Margaret would be right now. "Actually, I'm nearly finished with it. It should come out next year." The girl turned behind her and said, "Dad! Dad! Come meet KB Summers!"

Kate looked up as the tall, familiar figure stepped from behind the girl. She spurted out one word in disbelief, "Zach."

He was frozen, staring at her with wide eyes, and it seemed as if time stood still.

"Wait, you know each other?" the young woman asked incredulously, and Kate realized that this must be Chloe.

Zach found his voice, "We met a while ago—"

"This is fantastic. You have to join us!" Then Chloe turned to prod her dad. "Dad, give me the keys!" She turned back to Kate. "I have a writing journal. Would you please sign it for me?"

Kate nodded, her eyes still on Zach. He didn't break the moment and absentmindedly pulled a set of keys out of his pocket, handing them to the impatient Chloe without looking. She turned to race out the front door, and they were left alone.

"Kate," he exhaled.

She just nodded in shock as they both

laughed as they interrupted each other, "What are you doing here?"

He looked even more handsome than she remembered. His dark hair and strong jawline. Kate practically drank him in.

"Chloe just started her first year at UT and we are celebrating Christmas together down here."

Kate smiled. "Oh, that's fantastic! I'm so happy for her."

He looked at her expectantly.

"Oh, you won't believe this, but I've bought an Airstream and live at the same RV Park I wrote my novel in" she filled the gap.

"Unbelievable," he said. "I loved it, by the way. And I don't mind one bit being called your Dr. Wine." He winked at her. It was like no time had passed as they teased each other playfully.

Just then, Chloe came bursting into their moment and shoved her journal into Kate's hands.

"Oh, my gosh, this is amazing. Wait 'til I tell

my friends." She was feverish and completely unaware of the enormity of the whole moment. "Could we take a selfie?" she asked Kate.

Zach responded, still laughing, happy tears filling his eyes, "I'll do it." Chloe nestled right up next to Kate and put her arm around her while he held up his daughter's iPhone and said, "Ready?" his eyes sparkling.

Kate could feel the excitement of Chloe next to her, but she didn't dare take her eyes away from Zach's. "Ready," she said resolutely. He snapped a few pictures, then brought the phone down, their eyes still locked in unison.

"I've got to show you something," Zach said to Kate, and then turned to Chloe. "Find us a table and we'll be right back, sweetie." Chloe nodded as she was busy posting to her Instagram account.

He grabbed Kate's hand, which made her tremble in excitement as he pulled her through the courtyard and down the uneven sidewalks

on Main Street. They didn't let go as they maneuvered around the shoppers and revelers. He
was full of unexpressed excitement and Kate
was breathless when they finally arrived in
front of a storefront with brown paper covering
the windows.

Kate looked at him with a question, then
looked back at the windows. A large circular
logo was drawn on one with two letters, WW,
in the middle. She then read below it.

Winsome Winery—Coming Soon!

She opened her eyes wide and jerked her
head back to Zach to catch his laughter.

"Oh, my gosh! You did it!!" she exclaimed.

He pulled a set of keys out of his jeans pocket
and stepped forward to open the whitewashed
wooden door. He beckoned her to step inside
and Kate followed, stopping just inside the por-
tico darkness as he reached around her and
flicked a light switch.

Crisp white lights illuminated the space, and

Kate was breathless yet again. A long, hand-made oak bar top took up one side of the room, while beautifully carved tables and chairs were interspersed throughout.

The design was bright and clean yet traditional, with white walls and metal fixtures offsetting the light oak. It was gorgeous.

She turned to him. "This is amazing, Zach." She shook her head trying to take it all in. "I can't believe you did it—and yet this is exactly what I would have imagined from our conversations last year."

He took a deep breath and stepped toward her. "Kate. You inspired me. And after reading your book and seeing how you realized your dreams, I knew I needed to do the same."

He slowly held out his hands palms up, and she placed hers on top.

"I'm so proud of you." she said as they inched forward.

"Looks like we'll both be living out our

dreams here in the Hill Country," he said and her breath hitched as she caught his familiar scent.

He reached up and gently caressed the side of her cheek, tucking an errant blond hair behind her ear before closing the distance. He leaned forward to rest his lips against hers. Gently at first, then she pulled him closer as they grew more firm. Sweet and strong. A perfect fit.

They stayed that way for a while until finally pulling apart just enough that they could hold each other, with her head resting against his collarbone.

"I've wanted to do that since the first day I saw you." She could hear him through his chest.

Her heart was pounding loudly and she just nodded, feeling the strength and comfort of his chest and arms enfold her. At last.

As they pulled away and looked into each other's eyes, tears of joy glistened along the edges. Kate realized in that moment that the wait for perfect timing was worth every moment. All the pieces of the puzzle just fit together as they should. And it was finally seamless.

She ran her fingers against the stubble on his chin and said, "This is the most wonderful Cactus Christmas ever." They kissed again, as though they both knew that this was just the beginning of many more to come.

Letter from the Author

Dear Reader,

In 2018, I found myself going through my own bathroom floor moment and facing a difficult divorce. It challenged me to return to my faith and I was guided to Elevation Church in Charlotte, NC. Humbled to serve by coiling cables behind the stage and pushing the camera dolly back and forth, I opened my heart to heal. It felt like coming home. I had so much more I wanted to give, and I trusted that when it was time I would be able to do just that.

I wanted to believe again in a story of redemption and love, and I wanted to write that story to share with others. With those who may be going through a difficult time, facing a tough transition, or a life-changing choice: I know I'm not alone.

I began the Flipping Dreams podcast, to encourage others that it's never too late to change and grow. To leave your past behind and step into a brighter future. I interviewed and shared so many beautiful and heartfelt stories of people who had done just that and were now living their best lives. As I shared these stories, I also found healing and inspiration in the exchange.

At the end of 2020, during the difficult pandemic, I was staying full-time in my travel trailer in the Hill Country with my rescue pup, Dotty. Unable to be with family for the holidays, I chose to stay in Texas and be connected with my campsite community instead. I had time on my hands and I felt that maybe I was finally ready to write the story I longed to read and share.

So I began. Three months later, I had the bones of this book you are holding now.

Thank you for reading!

I pray it gave you hope. That you felt a connection with the characters and their struggles, and that you found joy in the arc when Kate goes through the difficult parts of her journey to find victory in the end.

I look forward to continuing their story in the next book of this series, Cactus Wedding (2022).

With deep regard,

Heather

Locations visited on the

Texas Wine Trail

Open Air RV Resort
Spicewood, TX
www.openairrv.com

Texas Heritage Vineyard
Fredericksburg, TX
www.texasheritagevineyard.com

Bingham Family Vineyards
Fredericksburg, TX
binghamfamilyvineyards.com

Longhorn Cellars
Fredericksburg, TX
longhorncellars.com

Fiesta Winery 290
Fredericksburg, TX
www.fiestawinery.com/about-290

Pontotoc Vineyard
Fredericksburg, TX
pontotocvineyard.com

Fredericksburg Winery
247 West Main Street
Fredericksburg, TX
fbgwinery.com

Lost Draw Cellars
Fredericksburg, TX
www.lostdrawcellars.com

Los Pinos Ranch Vineyards
Fredericksburg, TX
lospinosranchvineyards.com

Messina Hof Winery
Fredericksburg, TX
www.messinahof.com/hill-country-
fredericksburg

Grape Creek / Heath Sparkling Wines
Fredericksburg, TX
www.grapecreek.com

Ab Astris Winery
Stonewall, TX
www.abastriswinery.com

Hye Meadow Winery
Hye, TX
www.hyemeadow.com

Ron Yates Wines
Hye, TX
www.ronyateswines.com

For more information:

texaswinetrail.com
www.wineroad290.com
www.visitfredericksburgtx.com

⇒ Acknowledgements ⇐

Thank you to everyone who contributed to making this first book possible!

To my Flipping Dreams podcast community, thank you for sharing your stories and encouraging myself and others that it's actually possible to make those dreams happen. Thank you to the FabFive, and the Friends & Fiction community! Your weekly FB Live show fueled me through this process, and your tips and laughter were invaluable.

Thank you to Natasa, Dan, and the team at NY-BookEditors. I greatly appreciate you creating a place where self-published authors can access top editors to make their manuscripts be the best version possible. Thank you, Megan McKeever, for your very honest and encouraging feedback on my structural/line edits. You challenged me to create a better arc for Kate, and to make adjustments in the timeline and content that really tightened up the overall story and made it sing. Thank you, William Drennan, for your very thorough and accomplished copyediting. Your comments were insightful, and I am grateful for your expertise.

Thank you Ingram Spark for creating a place where self-publishing can be done in a most professional manner. You give power and agency to authors, and your tools and extensive guidance make it a smooth and enjoyable process.

To Christine, my Book Cover Whisperer, I am truly grateful for your talent. You got the essence of my story from the first version of the cover. Thank you for your beautiful artwork! To Victoria Horner, thank you for your delightful drawings. You captured each chapter so perfectly, and really added to the storyline.

Cindy Davie, thank you for reading my manuscript (not once, but twice!), and for giving your loving and thoughtful feedback. Our beautiful conversations and "wine-time" in your Airstream trailer were invaluable as I began writing and researching.

To my beta readers: Diane Hussey DeChillo, Kelly Ann, Victor Manuel, and Rebecca Burnett Lee. Thank you for taking time to read and give me your feedback! Your comments were so helpful and insightful, and I greatly appreciated each of your perspectives as I went into my final round of edits.

To my family, thank you for establishing a foundation of culture, arts, and literature, and for supporting all of my creative endeavors over the years. (And, of course, for instilling a deep sense of Texas pride and grit!)

It goes without saying that I am beyond grateful for the grace and mercy I am shown on a daily basis.

Finally, to the readers. Thank you for picking my book to spend your valuable time reading! I am grateful to each of you, and I hope that we meet at a book event in the future!

CACTUS WEDDING

A TEXAS WINE TRAIL SERIES

⇒ BOOK 2 ⇐

Heather Renée May

COMING IN 2022!

Sign up today for email notifications of pre-sale, book tour events, author meet & greets, and much more!

heatherreneemay.com/subscribe

About the Author

HEATHER RENÉE MAY is passionate about fourth quarter pivots, and delighted that she can finally channel her love of wine into something productive. She hosts the Flipping Dreams podcast, is a performing musician with two albums (Heather Ré), and a software engineer. She lives full-time in a 22-foot trailer traveling around the U.S. with her sweet rescue pup, Dotty. You can find out more on her website:

www.heatherreneemay.com